River Woman

By Martha Stinson

RoseDog Books
PITTSBURGH, PENNSYLVANIA 15238

RoseDog Books
585 Alpha Drive
Suite 103
Pittsburgh, PA 15238
Visit our website at *www.rosedogbookstore.com*

ISBN: 979-8-88527-930-7
eISBN: 979-8-88527-978-9

/ *Prologue*

The nurse tapped lightly on the door of apartment A-12 as she slowly pushed it open. Bright sunshine poured in through the opened curtain of the sitting room and it took a minute for her eyes to adjust before they focused on the frail figure sitting in the rocking chair looking out over the lush green lawn of Piney Woods Retirement Center. Mrs. Bradshire, a retired teacher and published author, turned her head when she heard her name called and smiled as she recognized the friendly face of Jean Smally, RN. Nurse Smally was her favorite of the nurses that her niece Sally had chosen to sit with her after the fall that had forced her into the hospital and later into the retirement center. It had been several months now, and the broken hip had not mended well, and the ordeal had left her weak and unable to walk without help. Even with the therapy which she painfully endured each day, she did not seem to be regaining her ability to maneuver on her on and was unable to return to her home. She had talked with her doctor and lawyer and they both had suggested that she consider Assisted Living.

Rebecca Bradshire, having always considered herself to be blessed with common sense and realizing that she was over seventy years old and would not likely ever be able to live alone again, had then agreed to settle her affairs and move into the newly built Piney Woods Retirement Center just outside of Charleston, West Virginia. Here she had a spacious five room apartment with a small patio from which she had a pictorial view of Big Walker Mountain and the New River. Although leaving her home near Glade Springs had been an emotional, almost a traumatic experience, she was adjusting nicely and considered herself lucky to be able to afford such a modern and comfortable place. She was able to fit her most treasured pieces of furniture into the new apartment and had enough storage space to accommodate the family mementos that she wanted to keep. She had private nurses around the clock and could afford to retain an attorney to see to her financial affairs. And she had Sally, her sister Mary Beth's only child and her favorite surviving relative. She had trusted her to see that everything left behind had been distributed according to her wishes.

Today, Rebecca was especially glad to see Nurse Smally because she felt up to going through more of the boxes still packed in a corner of the small bedroom she was using as an office, and Nurse Smally was always willing to oblige. As a matter of fact, she appeared to rather enjoy looking through the old picture and scrap books and reminiscing over trinkets and souvenirs that Rebecca had collected over the years. Now, Rebecca asks her to bring over an old hat box with a Legget's Department store logo, and place it on the ottoman in front of the rocking chair. The box was held together with scotch tape and was easily opened exposing a packet of cards tied together with a faded blue ribbon. There were Birthday, Christmas and Easter cards addressed to Mrs. Rebecca Bradshire, Route 3, Box 21, Glade Springs, West Virginia. Rebecca opened each one, read the names of the sender, then explained to Nurse Smally how each was related.

Under the cards, were several ladies' handkerchiefs, some with lace and others that had been beautifully embroidered with tiny flowers and vines. There was a faint smell of lilac as she separated each from the tissue paper in which it was wrapped. Beneath the handkerchiefs were letters, some with APO addresses from Viet Nam. These she said, were from her late husband Allan, who had served two tours of duty between the years of 1965 and 1968, and had made it back safely, only to have to fight a more horrible battle with cancer losing that war in late 1980. In the bottom of the hat box was a stack of notebook paper with a thin pink ribbon laced through the holes and tied into a small bow at the top. Rebecca gently lifted the booklet out of its nesting place, sat for a few minutes holding the yellowed pages in her lap, then told the nurse that she wanted to rest for awhile. Nurse Smally helped her to her bedroom and into bed before leaving the room, laying the booklet on her bedside table.

Rebecca closed her eyes, truly feeling very weary, but a few minutes later was reaching for the papers. She adjusted the lamp, put her glasses on and read the title page:

"My Memoirs"

by

Rebecca Lynn Carver

Miss Covington's 6th Grade

January 1946

River Woman

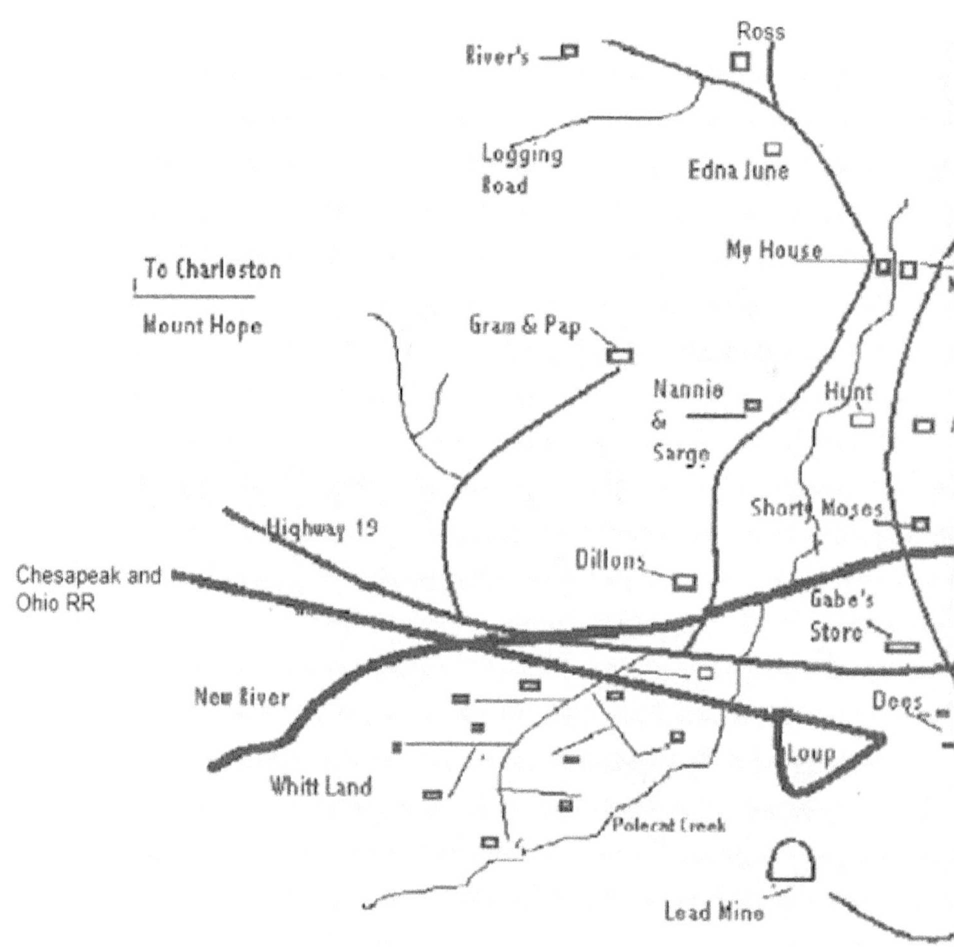

River's
Ross
Logging
Road
Edna June
To Charleston
Mount Hope
My House
Gram & Pap
Nannie
&
Sarge
Hunt
Shorty Moses
Highway 19
Dillons
Chesapeak and
Ohio RR
Gabe's
Store
New River
Dees
Loup
Whitt Land
Polecat Creek
Lead Mine

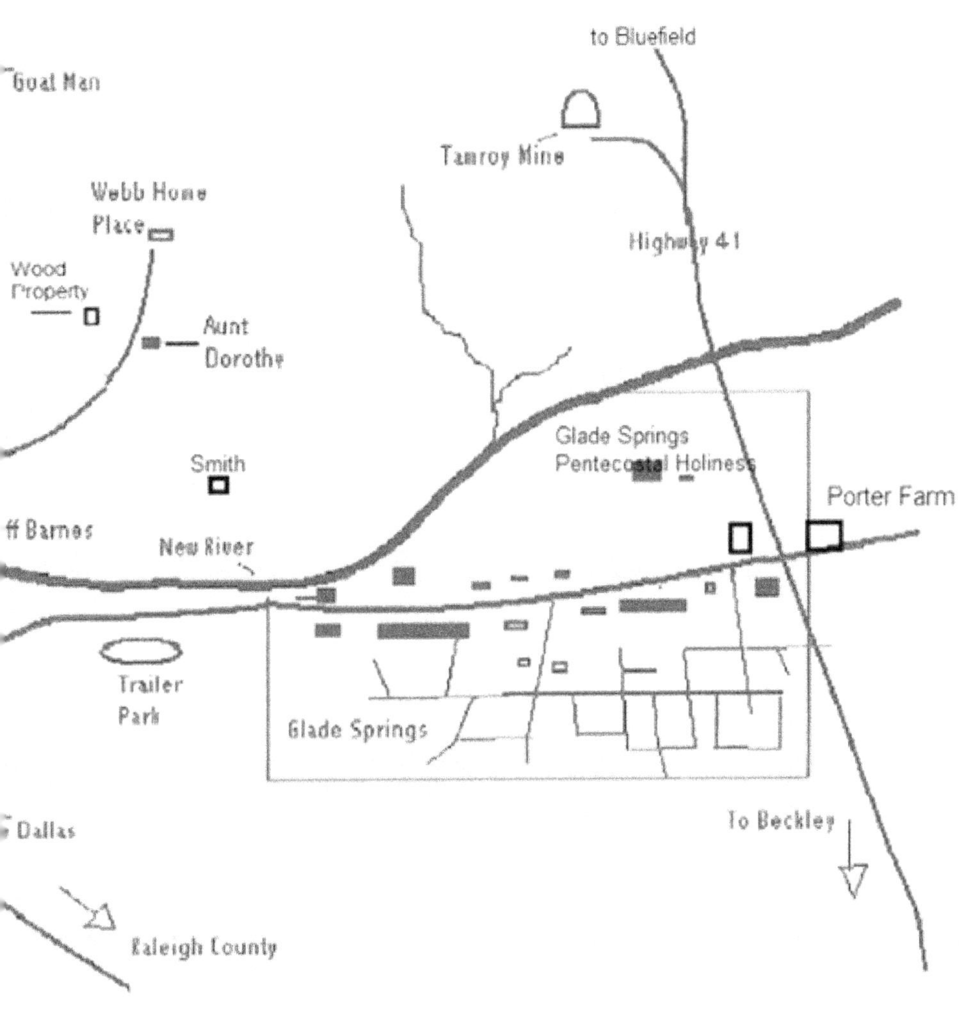

Goat Man
to Bluefield
Tamroy Mine
Webb Home Place
Highway 41
Wood Property
Aunt Dorothy
Glade Springs Pentecostal Holiness
Porter Farm
Smith
ff Barnes
New River
Trailer Park
Glade Springs
To Beckley
Dallas
Raleigh County

Chapter One

Mama yelled that the wood box was bout near empty as she came in the front room from the kitchen and warned that if anybody round this house wanted supper, somebody'd better bring in some wood. That, somebody I knowed was me, Rebecca Lynn Carver, just turned thirteen years old, and the oldest of the five Carver younguns. I was pacing the floor bouncing John Issac, my thirteen-month-old brother and the youngest of the Carver clan, on my hip as I walked back and forth. Mama took him and sat down on the day bed made up behind the heater and laid his head in her lap. She had warmed the sweet oil in a pan of water on the stove and putting her finger over the top of the bottle, lifted it up just enough to let a couple of drops go in John Issac's ear. He had had earaches ever since he'd been born. My sister Barbara Anne, younger than me by twenty-two months, came in from the bedroom holding the cotton out of the aspirin bottle that mama had sent her to find. Mama pulled off two little pieces of the cotton and put them in John Issac's ears to keep the sweet oil from leaking out.

I started out the back door, grabbed my daddy's old hunting jacket, and putting it on went out to get the wood. When the cold wind hit me in my face, I wished for the millionth time that my daddy would come home for something besides just making babies. We sure could use a man's help round the place, but Daddy stayed on the road. He'd bought him a 1938 Mack truck that had one of them bull dogs standing up on the hood like it was leading the way, and he was driving it for Lawson's Warehouse and Granary over in Beckly, and the only two-legged male on the place is John Issac. Another boy, Charles Garland, would've been six years old this year if he'd lived, but he'd only weighed about a pound at seven months and was just too little and weak to make it. Mama, me and my three sisters was left to keep the place going. We did alright as far as feedin the animals and we could gather eggs and milk the cow, but when it came butchering and planting time we had to depend on Mr. Robert Ross and his boys William Earl and Albert Paul who lived a couple miles up the cove, to kill the hogs and plow the fields. They'd work on halves. If we could raise two hogs in a year, they got one for helping kill and put up the meat from ours, and they could get half of the grain and vegetables raised on our land. Course, they never took half, just cause they was trying to help us out and they had enough of their own anyway. As far as keeping the barn and fences fixed, unless it was putting on a new roof or something like that, well that was left up to Mama and us girls, and believe me, we're nowhere near experts at carpentry and fence mending.

The wood pile is about twenty-five feet from the back door next to the smoke house. I stacked as much as I can carry and head back in. It would take about four trips to fill the wood box up, but I'd better do it now, cause the weatherman on our Philco radio said that the temperature was likely to drop into the twenty's tonight and I won't want to have to come out early in the morning to get in more wood. Mama can't carry in none. She's eight months along with child number six and even if she could've lifted it, she'd have to make about twice the trips to carry in the same as me. I'm big for my age like kin folk say, and I can do a lot to help out. I don't mind helping out, but sometimes I was just sick and tired of doing it all! Thinking like that always makes me feel kinda ashamed of myself cause I know that Barbara Anne and even eight year old Mary Beth both work hard helping Mama out around here, but sometimes it just makes me want to run away and hide and let somebody else do it for awhile. Well, I reckon that's just my daddy's blood coming out in me.

Chapter Two

My Gram Cole and Pap, Mama's mama and daddy, live over in the next hollow and I'm sure that Pap would come over and help us more if he was able. But the thing is, when he does come over he has to make sure that Sheriff Barnes ain't nowhere around before he drives the truck over to our place. Pap likes a little nip ever once in a while, and when he gets it, then he can't sit still, he gets the figgets, Gram says, and then he gets it in his head that he can still do work just like a young man. He jumps in that old 27 Ford truck and comes down that mountain running everbody and everthing off the road. The Sheriff has told him that if he catches him drinking again when he's driving, that he'll take that truck, and Pap, and put them in the jail house over in Glade Springs. Pap never got his driver's license neither, He said there weren't no use in anybody having to have a little piece of paper to prove they could drive when you could plainly see if they knowd how. Sheriff Barnes has told him he still had to get his license and says he'll get him for that, too, now that everbody that drives is suppose to have one. But most folks say that Sheriff Barnes probably wouldn't give Pap a ticket even if he did catch him. It would just depend on what mood he was in. As for Pap, he might say he's coming over to help us, but we know that he is just using that as an excuse to drive that truck over for a visit cause it's too far to walk to our place even if you come across the cove. And, I think sometimes he does it to get away from Gram and having work to do at his own place.

I reckon Pap's laziness is because he's just about plum wore out hisself. After all, him and Gram had nine younguns of their own, and he started working the mines over at the New River Coal Company from the time he was fourteen years old up until he got that bad cold that winter that wouldn't go away and the doctor said it was black lung disease. He was there when they had that big fire in 1910 that burnt up all of Mount Hope, and then when he'd get back everday, he took care of the home place too. So it's pretty plain, he could be tired. He had help, though. Four of his younguns was boys and all but one had stayed on the farm until they got married or started to work in the mines themselves and then moved out to their own place. Uncle Gerald, the one that didn't stay, run away when he was fourteen and joined the army. Folks say he came back a few times but I don't recall seeing him except when they brought him back a corpse. They laid him out in a box coffin in the front room of Gram and Pap's, and all the neighbors came by to sit up all that night. I wonder why folk did that, sitting there with a dead person. Surely they ain't thinking he might come back alive and get up and leave. I ain't never seen so much food, neither. Everbody that came brought something, and the folks sat around and talked and laughed about all the meanness Uncle Gerald had got into when he was a youngun. Course, it was all right now, cause it don't matter what you'd done once you're dead they all talked about you like you're some kind of a saint. I thought he was a big war hero since they'd said that he'd been in the army, but mama said he was killed in a hunting accident. She don't know it, but when I went out back to the outhouse that night, I heard Samuel Logan and Pete Collins talking about Uncle Gerald. They said that if he was killed in a hunting accident it must have been some woman's husband doing the hunting.

Chapter Three

Two of Pap's boys live just on the other side of Glade Springs and work the Tamroy mines, the other one lives over towards Mount Hope. He works for the Chesapeake and Ohio Railroad. They all have a bunch of younguns of they own and are too busy to do much visiting, so Pap does have to get wood in and keep things up pretty much all by hisself now. And, Pap and Mam had five precious little baby girls, but two of them that was twins died when they was real little of the fever. Two of the others married brothers and moved down to Low Gap, North Carolina. And then there is Mama, Emma Louise Cole, their youngest and their smartest they'd thought, until she married Daddy. How she got took in by that Garland Everet Carver, one of those good for nothing Carver boys from over in Wright's Cove in Greenbriar County, they could never figure out.. And when they tried to stop Daddy from coming around, he took my Mama and they eloped, all the way down to Bennetsville, South Carolina. I reckon Pap and Gram decided that they'd just have to make the best of it once they was married cause they didn't run Daddy off, and I reckon they could recall, too, when they was young and how it was with them.

Now Mama and Daddy when he was home, lived with Gram and Pap for the first couple of years cause I came along in a hurry and Mama was afraid to stay by herself over in the old packhouse that Grandpa and Granny Carver had fixed up and let them have to live in when they first got married. Besides,

Mama didn't want to live all the way over in Greenbriar County away from her mama and daddy. My daddy was already driving a truck then and staying gone away from home about four or five nights a week and my mama was not happy to be that far away from home with nobody in her family close by. But she'd been warned. There's this old saying around here, and folks swear that it's a true fact that if when you get married, if you change your name but not the first letter, that you'd marry that man for worse instead of better, and Cole and Carver both start with a C, so Mama should've knowed she was in for a hard time. And living in that pack house couldn't have been no worse for my mama.

I was a just a little over a year old and Barbara Anne was on the way, when Gram decided to move us out of her house. She was bound and determined that she was not gonna raise another family of young'uns and we was just somebody else to look after. I know Gram really didn't want to give daddy that house but she loved me and Mama and she wanted us to have a nice place even though she wasn't planning to be there to look out for us. Her brother Roland had died and since he hadn't never been married, he left his house and close to one hundred acres of rough land on the side of Big Walker Mountain in Fayette County, West Virginia, to his favorite sister. Now Gram had a way to help mama get her own place and a way to get us out of hers. But Gram would never put daddy's name on the deed.

Chapter Four

Gram told me that Daddy acted put out about it all at first, when she let us have the house, because he said that Gram and Pap though he wasn't able to take care of his family and that they was just trying to shame him, but then he stopped being mad real soon cause he found out it made it easier for him to stay away from home more. If folks said anything, he always reasoned that we didn't need him anyways, we had our own place and Gram and Pap to look after us, like his pride was hurt and he had to deal with it by staying gone. But he would show up from time to time though, like I said, long enough to keep Mama in the family way. He would bring money back with him, too, and a gift always turned up for Mama down at The General Store in Glade Springs every time Daddy found out she was expecting again. We got our Philco radio when Mary Beth was on the way. Mama never said much, but you could tell that she was tickled ever time she found out there was another package left over at the store. We do always have things, but, we don't see much cash money. Daddy made arrangements with Mr. Harvey Tyson so we can get what we need when he's gone if we run out. Mr. Tyson owns the General Store where Daddy almost always does his business, he don't do much with the company stores cause he don't work the mines. We get stuff like flour, sugar, and canned stuff in the winter when ours runs low, and we can get feed for the livestock. Mama makes most of our clothes and she can get the cloth, needles, and thread from Tyson's, too, and she'll buy us shoes when we need them. There're some folks that say Mama don't have a bad deal at all, with Daddy gone all the time she don't have to worry with him, and at least we don't go hungry or naked. Then there're those who say she's foolish, cause they say my daddy has a woman in every town from Charleston to Detroit, Michigan where he takes that truck. And they say it ain't no telling how many bastards there is strung out along that same route. I don't know nothing about no other young'uns, and I aint going looking to see cause I surely don't want no more brothers and sisters

Chapter Five

I took the last load of wood in the kitchen and dropped it over in the woodbox. Mary Beth, my favorite of my three sisters, helped me lay the wood straight. John Issac had finally settled down and Mama had put on her apron and come out to the kitchen to start supper. She took the eyes off the stove and put in some dry kindling to get the fire burning hotter. She had her bread bowl, flour and a can of lard on the little table beside the sink and Barbara Anne was greasing the bread pan. Mama would mix up the flour, lard and buttermilk, then knead it out in to ho'e cakes. This was faster than rolling out biscuits, course she'd fix them when company was coming, and I like ho'e cake better anyways because I'm partial to the fluffy inside of the bread. We was having fried pork chops, mashed potatoes, milk gravy, canned green beans, some of Miss Dee's homemade apple sauce and fresh churned butter with our ho'e cake bread tonight. Course us girls have got to go easy on eatings like this if we want to keep our figures.

It was getting dark by the time we finished eating, it gets dark early in the wintertime here in West Virginia, and Mama put more wood in the stove to heat water to wash the dishes and for us to take our baths with. We have electric lights, there's a light bulb that hangs down from the ceiling in every one of our rooms and there's some outlets on the the part that the light bulb screws in to where we can plug in a drop cord. One drop cord in the front room, some folks call it the sitting room cause that's where we usually stay, is hooked up to the radio, and there's one in the kitchen hooked up to our brand-new Frigidaire that Mama's buying on time from down at Marshall's Furniture Store in town. And when we do the washing, we unplug the Frigidaire and run that drop cord out to our washing machine on the back porch. We don't have running water or a indoor bathroom yet, but daddy has already bought the toilet.. It's sitting out on the back porch and I had to clean it out one time when Laura Kate thought it was ready to use just cause it was there, course Mama said I shouldn't have got so mad at her like I did cause she's still so little, and at least she used the toilet instead of messing up her breeches. We have a sink in the kitchen, too, and it has pipes that takes the water out under the house and we don't have to go out now and throw it off the porch, and Uncle Roland had built the back porch over the well, so it's easy to get a bucket of water in the kitchen or to fill up the washing machine and rinse tubs on the back porch on wash day. We don't have to go halfway across the yard like most folk do.

Me and Mama cleared the table, scrapped all the plates and threw the scraps out the back door for my two plot hounds, Roxie and Rattler, and stacked the dishes up to wash. Our Warm Morning Comfort stove has a water well built right in it, so any time there's a fire we have some warm water. Tonight, while Barbara Anne scalded the dishes and Mary Beth dried, I brought in the Number two wash tub off the porch and put warm water in so the little ones could take their baths. Laura Kate was almost four and loved to play in the water so I always put her in the tub first. She'd splash around until the floor was wet and wouldn't get out until the water was cold. Usually John Issac was next, but since he had an earache, it was best not to get him wet and chilled. I dressed them both in warm flannel pajamas with feet on them and took them to Mama in the front room. Then I had to mop up the water that Laura Kate had spilt. If you left any on the floor, it would freeze when the fire went out at night, and you could slip up and break your neck when you walked on it. And with Mama in her condition, we had to be really careful. She would sleep on the day bed beside the heater in the front room tonight with John Issac to keep him warm. We had two bedrooms, but there ain't no heat in either one and Mama knowed the cold air will make his ears hurt worse.

Barbara Anne, Mary Beth and me took our baths and washed our hair. We can only wash our hair in the wintertime if we have time to let it dry before going to bed. We'd catch our death, according to mama, if we went to bed with wet heads as cold as it was. But we had to go to school tomorrow and we wanted our heads clean. I reckon you could call us proud cause we liked to look and smell good. We got out our school clothes and our books and put everything on the long kitchen table where it would be easy to get to in the morning. When we had done all the work, we all got set down near the stove in the front room to let our hair dry and most nights we'd tell stories and sing songs. Mama played the auto harp and she would strum and we would sing "Sheepy and The Lamb", "The Banks of The Ohio" and some hymns, like Gram's favorite, "Farther Along". Then we would all pray before going to bed. Sometimes, if Mama was in the mood, cause the radio would have to be turned up pretty loud in the front room if we was to hear it in our rooms with the door closed, she would turn it on after we went to bed, and we would fall asleep listening to the likes of Hank Williams and Kitty Wells and the Carter family on WKXK radio station. And ever though WKXK was just over in Bluefield, I always thought that they sounded like they was a million miles away.

Chapter Six

Our old Rhode Island Red rooster was almost always crowing when the alarm clock went off. I reckon he was our back up, but there ain't no way nobody could've sleep through our Big Ben Westclock clanging. It was Barbara Anne's job to make sure it was wound up every night. Then she'd put it in a tin pan on Mama's washstand. When it'd go off, dead people couldn't a slept through that racket. Mary Beth was always the first one up. She was wide awake the minute her eyes opened and she'd jump out from under the quilts on the bed that me and her shared and tiptoe real slow like, so's not to stub her toes in the dark, out of our room through Mama and Daddy's and in the front room. It was warm in there cause Mama kept a fire going all night in that heater. She'd put a green log in before she'd go to sleep, and it would last til morning. Mary Beth snuggled under the covers with John Issac when mama got up, and talked silly baby talk to him to make him laugh. We all sorta favored him cause he was the only boy.

Mama pulled on that old chenille bathrobe of hers, tied it above her ballooned out belly and slipped her feet in her house shoes. The fire in the kitchen stove would have to be built from scratch, but it wouldn't be long before we'd smell coffee boiling and bacon frying. Me and Barbara Anne had got up, and left Laura Kate still sleeping in her and Barbara Anne's bed, and put our overalls and flannel shirts on as fast as we could. It was cold as ice in our bedroom.

Then we came out bare footed to the front room to get our brogans and socks that we'd left under the heater sos they'd be warm when we put them on. We found out that if you started off with warm feet, you didn't get near as cold.

We had to feed up and milk before going off to school, and it was still dark, it stayed dark longer in the wintertime, too, so I lit the lantern and got the milk bucket while Barbara wet a couple of old ragged towels in warm water to wash our cow's bag. Once we got to the barn, I put feed in the trough, cleaned the cows tits and sitting on the stool with the legs sawed off, put the bucket under her belly and started squeezing and pulling. Buttercup was an easy milker. She always stood still as could be and could give a full gallon bucket of milk twice a day, especially when she was fresh, and she had birthed a beautiful heifer calf just two months ago. Laura Kate named the calf Daisy, a fitting name I thought, cause they was both pretty as flowers. I partial though I just think Guernsey cows are the prettiest cows ever.

While I did the milking, Barbara fed up the rest of the critters and gathered the eggs from the nests in the part of the barn that we had fixed up for a chicken house. A big old oak tree, firewood for at least a year if we could get it cut up, had fell down last spring during that heavy rain that'd lasted about four days straight, and landed smack dab in the middle of the chicken coop. We got new wire from Tyson's and closed up a stall of the barn for the hens. They seemed to like it just fine. It was just like a big family in the barn. Cows, chickens, hogs and one old mule that had been Mama's Uncle Rolands, named Ruddy. He was about forty years old according to Pap and about as useful as Pap, , but we liked him too much to give him away, and besides, just how long could an old mule last. He didn't work no more though, he just stood around and took petting and food. At least, since he didn't have to do anything, it only took a little bit of grain to keep him up.

We had four hogs. Well, two full growed and a couple of shoats that we would keep for next year. Mr. Howard Langly had a pig farm down at Finchly near where New River and Wolf Creek forked, and since daddy hauled pigs for him sometimes in his truck, we could always depend on Mr. Langly to sell us a couple of runts at a good price. It didn't matter that they was runts, if you feed them good and love on them a lot they always seem to grow a right nice hog. But we couldn't get to liking the baby pigs too much. That happened one time with Barbara Anne when she was little. She fell in love with a tiny pig that she called Baby. She kept him in a cardboard box beside her bed and wrap him in an old crib blanket left over from one of us and fed him with a baby bottle. Then when it came time to butcher that full growed big old pig, Barbara cried so hard that Mr. Robert Ross had to take it up to his place and then tell her that he had traded it for this other hog that he had dressed out. Course, I knowed the truth, you can't tell one hog from another once't they're cut up in to hams and chops.

A couple of times we raised steers so we'd have our own beef, too, but beef ain't so easy to keep as pork. Most of it has to be kept in a freezer and the only freezer we have is that little box hanging down in the top of our new Frigidaire, and it wouldn't hold no more than a good size roast. We did manage to keep some of it in the spring house for a while through the winter months, it was good as a freezer as long as it stayed cold enough to freeze the top of the creek that ran thought it, but we winded up giving a lot of it away in the spring so it wouldn't go to waste. Now we usually just pick up a piece of beef or two when we go down to the market. It takes Barbara and me about thirty minutes or so to do up the barn work. Then we take the eggs and milk, and I always just happen to spill a little milk in a pan at the back steps that the hounds clean up for me, and go in to warm up and get ready for school. Mama and the little ones are bout done eating and Mama tells us to wash up and eat ours before it gets cold. Bacon and eggs and left over ho'e cake, sliced down the middle and toasted in the stove with fresh churned butter and some of Mama's blackberry preserves will keep us from being hungry until we get back from school.

Chapter Seven

I was real excited about going to school this morning, It was the first day back after Christmas vacation and I was tired of staying at home and I'd missed all my friends, especially my best friend Rachael. Besides, I couldn't wait to show off my new clothes. I loved getting dressed up for church and school anyhow. Mama is one skillful soul when it comes to sewing, just like Mrs. Geneva Hall down at Hall's One Hour Martinizers and Alterations says she is, and all us girls have some pretty things to wear. She can go into Charleston to the Woolworth's Store and pick out the hardest McCalls pattern there is, and in just a few hours peddling her Singer sewing machine, another gift for when Laura Kate was on the way, she'd turn out an outfit complete. And it was done as good as anything you'd buy over at Marlene's Dress Shop on Main Street in Beckley. My most favorite thing in the world is my gray wool cloak lined with red silk, well I don't know if it's real silk, but it looks and feels like it. It has a hood and deep lined pockets and I think I look just like one of them fashion model on the cover of "Women's Illustrated" magazine, when I've got it on. This morning I was going to wear my new black flannel skirt. It's so beautiful, real full and it comes down just below my knees and Gram had got me the softest pink sweater for Christmas. I pulled off my overalls and put on my crinoline slip and new skirt, then pulled that new sweater over my head, and, I even had some pink socks. I sure looked grown with that sweater on. I really have to wear a brazier now, not just because I wanted to wear it, and my bu-soms was standing out good under neath that sweater. Mama just shook her head from side to side right slow like when I twirled around to show her how I looked. We didn't always dress up in our Sunday best to go to school. Most of the time we wore warm pants lined with leggings and flannel shirts with our under shirts on but since it was the first day back after Christmas and we wanted to show off our new stuff, mama let us. But you know I have somebody special that I want to see me looking my best and so growed up.

Me, Barbara Anne and Mary Beth all go to school in Glade Springs. I'm in Miss Sadie Covington's sixth grade class, Barbara's in the fifth and Mary Beth's just in second grade. We catch the school bus on the dirt road that's about a quarter mile, least by my daddy's measurements, down below our house. William Earl Moss drives our bus. He's seventeen years old and is mean tempered and always acts kind of hateful. He likes bossing us younger kids around mainly to impress Edna June Harris. If we don't sit down when he says to, or if he thinks we're talking too loud, he'll report us to Principle Davis when we get to the school house, and we'll have to sit out in the hall near the office door until Mr. Davis gives us a note to take home. Us Carver girls know better than to come home with a note from the principal's office. Mama has done told us that we might not always make A's on our subjects, but that we'd better have all A's on conduct or we'd live to regret it.

Well, I almost always behaved good at school. The only time I ever had to go to the principal's office was that time when Miss Ammons, the librarian, caught me and Rachael Louise Abbott looking at naked pictures in the World Book Encyclopedias. It was our class's time to go in the library to pick out a book for a book report, and me and Rachael had already picked out ours, and was just killing time. Miss Ammons had always said that we could find really interesting things in the encyclopedias, and when we pulled out the very first one, the A book, and found pictures that had been took in darkest Africa, we got real interested. It had pictures of the natives with no clothes on, and this was the first time me and Rachael had ever seen full grown naked people, so we just had to look. We couldn't believe that women anywhere would go around with nothing covering up their busts, but we just could'n take our eyes off them men's "bodies." Well, while we was looking and snickering at them naked pictures, John Randall Nichols III, he was suppose to be the smartest boy in school, and he was the ugliest, came up behind us. He begged for us to let him see, and he even crossed his heart and hoped to die, that he would not tell. So we let him look, and that little hateful smarty pants went right to Miss Ammons. We saw her take a deep breath and put her hand over her mouth and then we heard "oh my goodness". Well, we knowed we was in for it then. Miss Ammons came back there and jerked the A Book encyclopedia off the table, we had closed it by the time she got there, but she had Mr. Perfect Nichols to open the book to the pages that we was looking at. Then she told us how nasty we was and grabbed me by my arm and Rachael by hers and marched us right down to Mr. Davis' office. She made us sit outside in the hall while she went in to tell Mr. Davis of our shameful actions. Mr. Davis didn't ever come out and talk to us, I think he was just too embarrassed, but he did write notes home to our folks.

I was scared to death to give that note to my mama. I just knowed she was going to send me after a switch, that's what she did when she was going to whip you, you had to go pick out your own switch and she'd tell us that if it was not big enough and she had to go herself, that she would get two and we would get two whippings. Course we didn't want to take a chance on getting two whippings, so we always got a right good size switch to start with. Then Mama asked me what was the name of the book that I had been looking at and I told her the A encyclopedia. She didn't say nothing else about the note, just told me to go about my chores. Well this scared me even more, cause Mama would sometimes make you worry about a whipping long before she got around to giving it to you. I couldn't even sleep that night, and when Mama drug Laura Kate and John Issac out, and him just a little bitty baby then, and got on the school bus with us that next morning, I just knowed I was in for a bad day.

It seemed like I was sitting out in that hall for hours that morning while Mama, Miss Ammons and Mr. Davis talked in his office. And all the other students knowed why I was out there, too. When they'd come down the hallway they would snicker like something stupid or make question signs by shrugging they shoulders. Well, they finally came out, and Mr. Davis had the reddest face I've ever seen on a man. Miss Ammons just looked mad. Mama told me to go on to my class and said that we would talk when I got back home, but for me not to worry. I found out later that she had told Mr. Davis that if he didn't want us seeing what was in them encyclopedias that he should take them out of the library. Mama wasn't happy that there was naked pictures where we could see them but she didn't blame us and I I didn't get no punishment from her. But some folks at school talked and laughed about me and Rachael getting caught looking at those naked pictures for a long time. And the gossips made sure that folks at the Glade Springs Pentecostal Holiness Church knowed about it, and we got a talking to by Sister Naomi Cox, our preacher's wife. Course, most of the ones at school just wanted us to tell them where them pictures was in them encyclopedias, and they became real popular books in our school for quite a while after that.

Rachael's mama wasn't quit so easy going as mine though. She gave Rachael a whipping for bringing home disgrace on their family and threatened to not let her play with me anymore if I was that kind of girl. But I guess she sort of just got over her madness, cause me and Rachael are still best friends. The only thing that really went wrong that time was that John Randall Nichols III had crossed his heart and hoped to die, and he didn't.

Chapter Eight

The bus was just coming around the bend at our road when we reached the bottom. William Earl stopped and opened the door for us. We got on and I looked around to see who was there already. Of course, Albert Paul and Polly, William and Albert's sister was there cause they get on the bus at the Ross' place where William parks it during the school year. The Barnette twins and their sister Mary who live at the very top of the cove, and the first ones picked up every morning and the last ones let off in the afternoon, was on. And Sam and Jessie Rivers. They lived in the next house down from where the Barnette's live. They're kin to us somehow, I think their mama and mine are third cousins, but they're so little that I don't pay much attention to them. Then William Earl picks up Edna June who lives between our house and the Ross' place. Edna June Harris is sixteen and has the reddest hair you ever saw. Everybody talked about what a temper she has that they say is just the way of redheads, and they say that if her and William Earl with his hatefull streak ever hookup, there'll be fights, good or bad enough, it's just on how you look at it, to buy tickets to.

Most of us on the bus have already seen a little of what their fights can be like when Edna was flirting with the Barnette twins to make William Earl jealous. Robert Lee and Thomas Jefferson Barnette are sixteen years old and as handsome as they can be. They're both big with muscles and if you weren't careful you'd get them all mixed up cause they looked so much alike. And they can be real charming when they're of a mind to be, too. But the thing about them Barnette twins is that they can dance like they've took lessons. Evertime there's a dance down at the Masonic Lodge in Beckly, all the girls want to dance with them. This is what the fuss was all about. We'd had a spring dance last year at the lodge and Edna had danced with the twins a bunch of times and William Earl Ross had not liked it one bit. So evertime Edna gets the least bit peeved at William she'll make eyes at Robert Lee and Thomas Jefferson Barnette. This one-time William had got so mad though that he put Edna off the bus just past our place and went all the way down to Highway 19 before he turned around and went back to get her. They broke up for at least a week. We all thought it was so funny though, cause we was late for school and that time William Earl had to take home a note.

This morning, Albert Paul was sitting on the very back seat with Edna. I was hoping that he'd talk to me, but he didn't say anything so I went about half way the bus and sat down in the outside seat. This way Barbara and Mary Beth would have to sit in another seat and I could save a seat for Rachael. Soon as I sat down, I started hoping real hard that the bus would hurry and warm up so I could take my coat off. I wanted everybody to see my new outfit, and I especially wanted Albert Paul to see how my pink sweater fit. I've been in love with him ever since I can remember, but he is fifteen going on sixteen and I'm just twelve, so he don't won't nobody to think that he likes me. And I don't think he ever thought much about me either until last winter when we was killing hogs. Like I told you before, the Ross' help us out when our daddy ain't at home. The men do the killing, scalding and scrapping and then bring the hogs in the kitchen quartered up. Then they'll cut them to make the hams, shoulders and chops, because anything that has a bone in it is too hard for most women to cut up. Then the women take over to work the sugar curing or salt into the meat. Hams, shoulders, bacon, side meat and hog jaws are rubbed real good and wrapped in brown paper and put into flour sacks and hung in the smoke house to cure. Then we cut up the chunks of meat that we put in the sausage, these chunks are mostly the scraps cut off the choice pieces of meat like the hams, then we season and grind it and packed it in hog guts. All of the fat meat's cut up in little pieces and put in big pots so that the grease can be cooked out to make lard, and the cracklings, thats what they call what is left over after all the fat cooks out, can go in cornbread later on.

Most of the hog meat's put up for later, but the one thing we always have the day of slaughtering is fresh pork liver, and lights too, if you liked them, with gravy and onions. Hog killing's a lot of hard work, and everybody that's big enough has to help, unless you're deathly sick or if you're a woman and having your monthly flow. Old folks swear that any of the hog meat that gets touched by any unclean female will spoil, so they wouldn't let me get nowhere near to them hogs. Course Albert Paul, having a mama and sister of his own, knowed bout this and when I couldn't help out he knowed the reason why. That's when he started looking at me and grinning and talking to me when we weren't around William Earl or Edna. Even though he thought of me as almost a woman, I was still just twelve to his fifteen, and he knowed that everbody would be funning him about robbing the cradle if he was caught talking like he was interested in me. But I knew deep in my heart that we would get together one day, all I had to do was wait a bit and keep him looking.

Chapter Nine

After me and Barbara Anne and Mary Beth get on the bus, we pass by the house where Nannie Mae Simmons O'Brian and her son Sarge lived up until just a few months ago. Nobody has got on the bus here in a long-time cause all of old Nannie's younguns is dead except Sarge and he never went to school. Use to, ever time we'd come down the road when it was warm enough, Nannie and Sarge would be sitting out on their front porch in their rocking chairs, and they'd always wave at us. My Gram says it's a shame about Nannie. Of all the folks she's even knowed, she thinks that Nannie probably had the roughest time of it. She got married to Orville O'Brian back in 1902. He worked over in the coal mines in Mount Hope and lived in one of the mining houses just outside of town. Nannie was helping out at the boarding house, cooking and cleaning and such, and Orville took a liking to her. Seems she was right much older than him but that didn't matter, after all, pickings was somewhat slim way up here in the hills and Orville had come all the way over here from Ireland or somewhere like that, and it was just too far for him to go back just to find a wife. So, Orville started courting Nannie. Now, Nannie had been married before to a man named Gus, that's all I ever heard was just Gus, and they'd had two youngouns, both of them boys, before he got killed in the mines when there was a explosion of some sort. After he'd been dead awhile, she married Ralph Simmons and they'd had two younguns, too, two more boys, and then

Ralph Simmons got killed in the mines when a vain flooded. Well, I reckon Nannie had figured by now that her luck with husband weren't so good, and she started working at the mining house to make some money. She was raising her youngouns right along, the two oldest boys had already got old enough to work the mines, when Orville moved in the mining house. Folks say that Orville wouldn't leave Nannie be, that once he decided that he was going to marry her he stayed after her even with her saying no. Well, finally he wore her down and she told him she would be his wife.

Gram says that Nannie had to be at least thirty-five years old when her and Orville got married and she figured that Orville was around twenty. Some folks talked about how Nannie was old enough to be Orville's mama, but the two of them seemed to get on real well for a while. Nannie and Orville and two of Nannie's four boys moved over here from Mount Hope and built them this house just down from where our place is. After they had been married about a year or so, along came Sarge. Now, his real name is Patrick Elgin O'Brian, but he gave that name of Sarge to himself when he was about ten years old, cause he was always pretending that he was a sergeant in the United States Army. What I know is that Sarge is just a little slow and stutters when he talks, so a lot of folks made fun of him. Even his own daddy would smack him up side his head and call him names like you'd never think a daddy would do, and he wouldn't take little Patrick no where with him cause he was ashamed for folks to know it was his. And he called Nannie bad names and beat her up pretty bad some times. Gram says somebody ought to have took that man out and beat some sense in to his hard head, anybody'd that'd treat his own wife and boy so bad. But Nannie loved Sarge just like she'd loved all the rest of her young'uns. And, he was different so she always kept him close to her side to protect him from the folks who'd poke fun at him. Ever where you saw Nannie, you saw Sarge. She carried him on her back, he was big enough that his feet touched the ground, and you'd see her toting him, plum up till the time when he became a sergeant in the army and figured that he was too grown up to be toted. She was so afraid that Sarge would get teased and hurt that she wouldn't even let him go to school. His big brothers taught him how to read and write a little, and they read him lots of stories, especially stories in the comic books about the war. Sarge loved him some of them comic books, and that's how he knowed about army people.

When Sarge was twelve-years old, his daddy and all his brother was working over in the mines at Mount Hope and there was a cave in and everyone of them was killed. Now, folks say that Nannie just lost her own mind right then and there, not because of Orville, Lord knows she was probably glad to be rid of him, but losing all those boys, and all at one time too, was more than a body could stand. She still had Sarge, but now folks said her mind wasn't no better than his was. Well, there they'd been all these years since, just Nannie and Sarge sorta looking out for one another. Ain't nobody sure just how they've made it, but they did. Even when Nannie was eighty years old and Sarge was in his forties, ever where you'd see Nannie, Sarge was still right there beside her. Course they had got to where they didn't go much of anywhere, you didn't hardly ever see them out of the cove, but we'd see them walking and just about evertime we come down the road, they'd still be sitting out on their front porch in their rocking chairs.

I heard Mama and Gram talking again just the other day, about that lady from the West Virginia Department of Social Services that had been to see about Nannie and Sarge and told them that she was taking them to the nursing home over in Charleston. Mama said that when that lady was talking to them, that she talked just like they was both little younguns, telling what a fine place they was going to. Well, seems like everything was going on pretty good, the lady had put Nannie and her things in her car and then tried to get Sarge in. Mama said he pulled out that stick of his that he had made like a sword when he tied a handle to it with baling wire and told that lady that he was a sergeant in the United States Army and she'd better not touch him or the MP's would come and get her and put her in the brig. He told her that the only way that he'd go anywhere would be if the Colonel was to send the MPs with orders for him to go serve his country over seas. After a couple of hours, they went and got some deputies, it wasn't Sheriff Barnes, though, it must have been some deputies from Charleston, and since they had on uniforms, I reckon Sarge thought they was the MPs, and he left with them. Now their house is just sitting there. It's still got their things in it but Mama says it's doubtful that either one of them will ever step foot on the place again. I ain't heard nothing else about Nannie and Sarge in a while, but I do hope they're doing all right over there in the old folks home.

The last house on our road, before we turn on to Highway 19 is the Dillons, or "dirty Dillons" as they're called to their backs, and sometimes to their faces when they get into it with the Whitts. Everybody says old man Dillon's lazy and sorry as sorry can get cause he won't work a lick at a decent job. Some said he ran moonshine, but Gram said they weren't rich enough for that. Folks that made or run shine always had some money. And, even if they spent some time on the chain gang, they'd still have made enough before getting caught for their family to live pretty good 'til they got out. Mr. Dwayne Lee Dillon had spent some time on the road, and they say his family liked to have starved to death. If it hadn't been for Dwayne Lee Jr. and Jasper knowing how to hunt, it's only a wonder just what might have happened to the rest of them while he was gone.

Some of the Dillon clan has black kinky hair and dark skin and green eyes and they was called mixed, and some go on to say that they was mixed amongst themselves, too. Sarah Jane, the oldest of the Dillon girls who is just a couple years older'n me, already has a baby and another one on the way that folks swear has been fathered by old man Dillon himself. Them Dillon young'un's don't have no mama cause she had died in childbirth when that last one was born. They're called trash, but I'm not quite sure just what that means, cause it looks right nice around their place they mostly always look clean. I haven't talked to Sarah Jane in a long time cause the only time I ever saw her anyways was on the bus and at school, and she quit school when I was in the fifth grade. I liked Sarah Jane, though. It didn't seem to matter that I was younger than her, she would sit with me on the bus or on the playground, and I never heard her say a mean word against nobody. She always just talked about going to New York City when she got old enough to leave home.

She was the first person to show me "Women's Illustrated" and "Saturday Evening Post" magazines with pictures of those fashion models in them. That's what she said she was going to be when she got to New York City, a fashion model. She could have been one too, if she could've gone. She's about the most beautiful girl I've seen anywhere around here. She has the longest, silkiest, blackest hair and her eyes are turquoise colored like the jewelry that the Mingo Indians over in Kanawha County wear. She knows how to stand straight and could walk with books on her head, that's what models did she told me, and whenever she walked around town she was always being whistled at and the men and boys couldn't keep their eyes off of her. She didn't have many girl-friends though, and the women round here didn't seem to like her and didn't want their men folk talking to her, so I guess that's why she spent time with me. But, I had to quit talking to her once she got disgraced and I know for pretty sure that I'll never get to talk with her again cause nobody knows for sure where she is now. Some say she left town the same day that Mr. Eric Rodgers left his house and car dealership out on the corner of highway 19 and highway 41. People have said that ever time Mr. Rogers would see Sarah Jane out walking, he would try to talk to her. I don't know cause mama had told me that she'd beat me half to death if I had anything to do with Sarah Jane Dillon once she was disgraced. She's told me over and over again that you're knowed by the company you keep, and that no decent person would want anything to do with the likes of the Dillons. But I know deep inside me that if I ever got the chance to talk to Sara Jane that I would.

Chapter Ten

After we pick up the Dillons and get to the bottom of the cove, we make a left
turn onto Highway 19. If you turn right, you only go a little ways and you'll
be at the line where they separated out the ones who go to school in Mount
Hope, not over in Glade Springs with us. The first three stops we make on
Highway 19, we pick up Whitts, or some kin of theirs. Every mountain community has a family like the Whitts. Clannish is what Gram calls them and
says that they're a mean bunch. They all stay right close together all the time
even after they're grown. All the girls brought their husbands back to their
daddy's place after they was married. and them and their brothers had all kinds
of little houses built all over old man Caleb Whitts land. You didn't mess with
the Whitts, neither. They're bad and they'd fight you in a minute, even the
girls. Some say they've got something to hide, maybe from the law, and Pap
says that he wouldn't be one bit surprised if they was making moonshine again
down on Polecat Creek where it runs through their place. Mr Whitt has already been in the pen and his two oldest boys was on probation for making
and hauling whiskey. Folks say that's how they got hold to all that land they
have. But they ain't suppose to have no way to cook up the mash now cause
they got caught and their still was tore up. Pap laughs, but swears it's the God
honest truth, that when them revenuers found Mr. Whitt's liquor still and
blowed it up, that the moonshine ran down in Polecat Creek, and when the

cows come up to the barn that night, that they was drunk as hoot owls. Says it was plum pitiful to hear them cows bellowing and to watch them walk like their knees was gonna buckle right up under neath their bellies.

Course nobody knows for sure just what them Whitts is up to cause you can't get close to them. Nobody better be caught anywhere on their place and you don't even try to be nice or friendly with them cause they picked and chose who they want for their friends themselves. I'm sure glad that I'm not one of the chosen ones. I'm sorta scared of the Whitts myself. I've seen them pick fights with the Dillons and the Dees that lived down the road from them, but so far they'd not got it in for me or my sisters. The girls wore big shirts and overalls to school just like the boys did and their brown tie up shoes would always be red because of the mud on them. There was a lot of red clay on Big Walker Mountain, and when it rained, it would stick like glue, and I don't think the Whitts ever tried to get any of it off of their boots. Once the mud dried, you could track a Whitt anywhere'd they go.

They did crazy things too. Me and Pap had to go get some stuff from Mr. Tyson's General Store one summer day, and when we passed by where the Chesapeake and Ohio railroad crosses over New River, some of them Whitts was out there jumping off the trestle in to the river. Pap says that trestle is over 50 feet high and that there's rocks in the bottom of that river and he can't figure why they didn't get killed. But I reckon it's because of their faith. They all go to church together up in Burr's Cove to that little plank church where it's told that they handle serpents and they have faith enough that they won't get bit that they'll let them snakes crawl all over them. One time I asked Pap about how did they do it, to not get bit when they picked them serpents up. Pap said that Whitt's is meaner than a whole bunch of rattle snakes and that the snakes was afraid of them. I can see it though, where if you have faith not to be afraid to pick up rattle snakes and river moccasins with your bare hands, that jumping off a trestle that's 70 feet high wouldn't bother you too much.

The worst thing I could see about them Whitts, though, was that they chew tobacco, the girls, too. Their jaws would be poked out like they was going to bust and they'd have brown juice running out the sides of their mouths and if they had to spit, they'd just spit out the windows of the school bus leaving those brown streaks all the way down the side . Even in the winter, if they had to spit they'd open a window stick out their head and let it go, freezing everybody to death. I was sure hoping that they wouldn't have to spit today, because I was still waiting for the bus to get warm enough for me to take off my coat.

Chapter Eleven

After picking up the Whitts, the bus makes a left turn at the crossroads of Highway 19 and Logan's Cove Road, to go back up the mountain. I saw Marsha Foster looking out the door of her daddy's place, Gabe's Store, when we made the turn. She'd get on the bus when we come back down out of Logan's Cove and stop in the store yard. Her daddy's Gabrial Foster, and they had their house built right on to the back of that store. I always wondered what it would be like to just get up from what you're doing and walk right through a door straight in a store to get whatever it is you want. I thought she was the luckiest person around. Course they didn't sell near the things that you found down at Tyson's. They didn't have clothes or dishes or hardware and stuff like that, it was mostly food like bread and pork and beans and drinks. The best thing though, was ice cream and candy. Marsha always had candy and chewing gum in her lunch bag and when we let her off the bus, she mostly got off in the afternoon before the bus went up the cove, and she'd be standing out on the porch eating ice cream on a stick when we came back down. She'd wave real friendly like, but really what she wanted was for us to see her with her ice cream.

They had a telephone, too, something that most folks in our area didn't even know how to use. Mama had talked on that one at Gabe's Store though, when Sheriff Barnes had come to the house to get her and Pap cause the Sheriff over in Roanoke, Virginia had called the jail house looking for somebody that was kin to Gerald Cole. He took them down to Gabe's store to make the call and it was when they found out that Uncle Gerald had been killed. Mama had been the one to talk to the sheriff. She said Pap had said that he was getting so hard of hearing that it would be better for her to do it, but Mama said later that she thought Pap was scared of that telephone cause he wouldn't even touch it. So she did the talking on it and she said it sounded like that sheriff was just over in the next room. Course, nobody much around here likes getting telephone calls as it almost always means that somebody has died or maybe something else bad has happened.

Well, me and Marsha was friends for awhile even though she had those biggity ways about her because of her telephone and her ice cream. We started school the same year, but when I turned thirteen, she was still acting like she was ten years old and that was way to young for me to want to fool around with her.

William Earl had to gear down the bus to get it started up Logan's Cove. It was a lot steeper with the road being cut straighter up the mountain than most, and there was nowhere for him to turn the bus around until he got to the very top. This is where Marion Marshall Moorefield, or "Goat Man" as most folks call him, lives. He lets the school bus turn around here, cause it's the only place wide and flat enough for William to pull the bus in and then back it straight back enough to turn and head down the mountain. But that was all we could do. Goat Man would stand on the porch of his old run down house and watch to make sure that the bus did not spend any more time than it had to there. Folks say that Sheriff Barnes had to talk, course I think he probably bribed or threatened, Goat Man into even letting the bus come on his property at all. He'd always, well, long as I had knowed about him anyways, lived at the top of Logan's Cove with his goats, a few chickens, a pony and a big old shaggy dog. He lived like a hermit with no running water or electricity in that old shed he had been living in since he'd come back from the war. He wouldn't live in the house that he had fixed up so nice and pretty for Nancy and of course she the had took her Cadillac car with her when she left. He didn't even have a car or truck. Here it was 1946 and he still hooked up that pony and cart to come down to town when he brought his milk and cheese in to sell it, or when he needed something from the store.

He always smelled just like them goats, too. One time in Penny's Diner, this little cafe in town, when Mama and us was in there getting a Orange Crush, he came in and sat down right next to us. Mama acted neighborly and said hey to him, but he just looked at her and sorta shook his head up and down a bit and then kept staring down in his cup of coffee.

Laura Kate pinched her nose together and Mama smacked her hand while me, Barbara Anne and Mary Beth giggled and almost gagged. It didn't take us long to finish up them Orange Crushes and get out of there neither.

It's strange though. Gram has known Marion Moorefield ever since they was youngouns together, and she says that his folks was always decent enough and they was real friendly. She says they found a gold mine on their place too, and left him well off when they both died of the flu in just a few days of one another. And she said when he growed up, he was one good looking fellow. So he had his handsomeness and money too, and all the girls around here were after Mr. Marion Marshall Moorefield. He wasn't about to be caught by none of those country girls of Fayette County, though, cause he only had his eyes on Miss "Fancy" Nancy Flemming. a big city girl from Charleston, our Capitol City of West Virginia. He met her at a social gathering over in Pixly when she was visiting with her aunt. He wouldn't even talk to the girls around here after that, but just chased after Miss Flemming and was always buying her fancy jewelry and stuff. Well, he finally talked her into marrying him, and then he brought her back up to his place to live. But then, he ended up in the war with Germany not too long after they was married. I think it was in about 1912, that's what Pap thinks anyways, and when he came back home from the army, that gold mine was empty and Mrs. Nancy Flemming Murphy had left and took everything she could carry. They say the only thing that was still there on his place when he got back from serving his country was the house, a shed and barn. Some say he went wild as a bear, and that he ain't never had a human friend since. He wouldn't even live in the nice house he had built for her but left it to fall down. He lives in the shed there on his property. The way that I'm thinking though, is that he might have got the best end of the deal after all. I can think of lots of animals, like Roxie and Rattler and Buttercup and Daisy, that I would rather have as friends in place of some of the people I know.

Chapter Twelve

Coming on down the mountain, after leaving Goat Man's place, the first house we pass belongs to Miss Claire Thompson. Miss Clair is older'n Gram, but that little old lady can move about quick as a jack rabbit. I had to fetch her when John Issac was borned, and when I yelled across Little Creek that runs down the hollow between her place and ours that Mama was birthing, she came across that hollow and creek so fast, I could have sworn that she actually walked across that water without stepping on the stones and didn't sink one inch. She always wore her long cloak and carried a homemade basket full of sure fired cures for about anything that a person'd ever get. Some of the new folks down on the highway claim that she's a witch cause she goes around in that black cloak chanting and humming songs while she walks about the mountain digging up roots and picking herbs and mushrooms and ginseng and bloodroot. They all just turn they heads and walk away talking bad about crazy old Miss Clair. But that just shows how ignorant they are. Everybody born and bred in these mountains knows that medicine is mostly made from plants and that only special folks have the sight and the gift of curing and know how to use the medicine plants for what they was meant to be used for.

Course Reverend Bentley Martin from over at The First United Methodist Church in Anstead tells folks that Miss Clair ain't no more than a moonshiner cause she uses home brew as the main ingredient in her potions. That's just because most of the folks who take her medicines ends up feeling so good that they come down off that mountain laughing and dancing about. Even the Whitts call on Miss Claire when they're ailing. She's the only person not belonging to their family that can come and go as she pleases on their land. It does make a body wonder about things though, maybe the Whitts are making shine and it could be that since Miss Claire's got the sight, that she knows about them making it. Then they let her have some to mix in with her plants and herbs so she want report them to the revenuers. But, I'm not about to ask none of them about that.

Now, as much as I truly believe that Miss Clair has the sight and gift of healing, even I have to snicker a little bit when some of the women folks tell tales about the potions and talisman's she's made for them. They say she can cast a love spell so powerful that it makes the one you want come begging at your feet. Seems to me like she'd a made one for herself, though. Miss Clair ain't never been married. Gram says it's because all the men around here's afraid of her powers, but Pap says it's because she's always acted queer in the head and was ugly to boot. He says that folks have always claimed that Miss Claire was some kin to "Mad" Ann Bailey from over near Charleston. The Indians back then called Mad Ann the "Great White Spirit" cause they said she had an evil spirit about her. I think they was just puzzled about her cause it was said that she could ride horses and shoot guns as good as any man and that she weren't afraid of nothing, not even them Indians. And others tell that Mad Ann surived all those years cause them were afraid of her too. Said she'd stand right there and scream at them Indians and they would turn and run away. Anyway Gram will hold her breath when Pap talks like this about Miss Clair and Mad Ann , and looks about like she expects for the earth to come tumbling down around them. But so far, I guess Miss Clair's sight can't focus in as far as Pap's place, cause the world is still standing. I might just have to go up to see her soon myself and have her make me up one of them love spells so Albert Paul will come begging at my feet.

Chapter Thirteen

The next house down the cove from Miss Clairs on the left hand side is where the Jacob's live. They're a young couple that have only been married for a few years. He works in the coal mines, too, and she stays home with their poor little crippled baby boy. Gram says that it'll never grow up and that it would be a site better for everbody if he would just go on home to be with Jesus. That would surely save a lot of misery for him and his folks, she says. I ain't never seen it but twice. One time at the Glade Springs annual picnic and when we was in Doctor Smith's office in town when Mama had to go for a check- up, to see if her own baby was doing alright, and Catherine Jacobs was in there with that pitiful little thing. She had me to hold it while she took off her coat and I just couldn't help looking him all over good. He had the sweetest looking little face, but his head looked like it was way too big to go with his little bitty body and his skinny little arms and legs was bent in all different directions. It looks like if you'd just take his feet and hands and pull out real hard that they'd stretch and straighten out.

Now nobody knows for sure why he was born that way. Some say it's because Walter Jacobs is kin to them inbreeding Dillons and nobody knows for sure what's in their backgrounds. But then Miss Claire, she's a granny midwife, too, said that Catherine marked that baby when she went to the state fair in Fairlea, just south of Louisburg, when she was expecting it and went in to look at that two headed calf. Catherine says that's not so, that she didn't do nothing but glance at that thing and she didn't even think it was real anyhow. She says that the doctors told her that it's just something that happens sometimes and there ain't nothing nobody can do about it. My Aunt Dorothy's been up there to talk to them about bringing him over to our church, Glade Springs Penticostal Holiness Church so that Brother Cox, our preacher, can anoint that baby with sanctified oil and pray for his healing. She tells about seeing God perform miracles of all kinds and she says that if the Jacobs will join with the Christian people and they all have faith that it can happen, that that baby can be made just as normal as anybody else. I don't know if the Jacobs go to church anywhere, but so far, Aunt Dorothy ain't been able to talk them in to coming over to ours either. I really believe that baby can be made whole, just like Aunt Dorothy says and I sure hope that The Lord will heal it soon, cause I ain't never seen nobody look so sad all the time as Rachel Jacobs does.

Chapter Fourteen

Just across the road from Walter and Catherine's house is where Walter's sister May Ella and her husband Roger Hunt live. May Ella is about the same age as Rachel, and her and Roger already have three youngguns. Two girls and a little boy named Simon. The oldest girl, Jenny Lou, is one of the smartest young'un's you've ever seen and she can sing like a song bird. They have her get up in front of their church, they go to the Baptist Church on Hill Steet in town, on Sunday mornings and sing hymns for the rest of the folks. She is just six years old and can't read too much yet, so somebody has to tell her the words, and she can remember them songs too, after only hearing them read to her just once or twice. Then she rares back and lets it go. Now, Walter's best friend, Shorty, everybody calls him Shorty cause he's a midget. Course ain't nobody surprised that he's a midget cause there' s some that claim that he's kin to the Dillons and you know about them. But he can play a guitar as good as any of the people you'll ever hear on the Grand Ole Opry. He has a guitar that is as tall as Shorty Moses himself when you stand it on its end, and he can sing harmony right along with Jenny Lou. It is some kind of pretty to listen to them two sing. The neighbor people say that Jenny Lou should go to Nashville, Tennessee and sing for one of those record companies since she has the voice of an angel, but Roger and May Ella say they can't afford to go off and leave their other young'un's just so Jenny Lou can sing. Besides, if Roger was to go off and leave his job in the mines, somebody would be sure to get it before he got back with so many coming back to the hills now that this war's over, and then they wouldn't have no way of making a living.

It's a shame though, that nobody but the folks here abouts will ever hear Jenny Lou sing, with her sweet clear voice and her not the least bit shy, neither. The first time I ever heard her sing, we was at the Glade Springs Annual Picnic over at that big field in the bottom that runs alongside New River just east of town. Everybody had brought their picnic lunches and there was fresh squeezed lemon aid and homemade ice cream that Mrs. Mable Osborne, the wife of Ezra Osborne who runs the Flour Mill and Ice Plant there on the river, had made. After everybody'd got done eating, all the folks that could play music got their instruments out and gathered under one of the big oak trees in the field. There was guitars, a fiddle, a banjo, a wash tub bass, spoons and Mama had her autoharp. I can remember that day clear cause it was a special one. My daddy was there with us and he sat there grinning at Mama, while she was playing and singing, like he was the proudest husband that there ever has been.

After a while, Shorty picked up Jenny Lou and stood her on a stump where one of the big oak trees had been cut down. He started playing his guitar, Mr. Dees started sawing on his fiddle, and Jenny Lou started singing "Amazing Grace How Sweet the Sound". The other young'uns' around even quit their playing and came over to listen to her. After she had got through, everybody started begging her to sing it some more. Then when Jenny Lou started with "Amazing Grace" again, everybody started singing with her and Shorty. It made cold chills run up my spine it was so pretty. That was one day when it didn't matter what church you went to in town, everybody felt the spirit of the Lord as we stood there singing together. Jenny Lou is a friendly little thing, too. When the bus stops to pick her up, she's in the first grade at Glade Springs School, she just smiles at everybody when she gets on. Maybe it's meant for Jenny to just keep her talent here on Big Walker Mountain for now, but I bet if the right person ever comes through here and hears her singing, she'll be famous someday.

Chapter Fifteen

The next house and the last one before we get back down to the crossroads at Gabe's Store, is where "Shorty" William Elmer Moses himself lives. He's ever bit of three feet, eleven inches tall, but as I told you before, he might be some kin to the Dillons so there ain't no wonder that he could be like he is. I've seen Shorty around for as long as I can remember. As a matter of fact, he's the first afflicted person I ever saw. But even though Shorty is kin to the Dillons you'll never hear nobody saying nothing bad against him. He goes to church over at the Glade Springs Pentecostal Holiness Church, the same church that we go to, and he never misses a meeting. He's there on Sunday morning for Sunday School and Preaching, Sunday night for service and Bible study and on Wednesday nights for Prayer Meeting if it's not held at somebody's house. And if it is at somebody's house, he's there too. He's been doing this all of his life. When he was just a little bitty baby, his mama left him at the door of the Glade Springs Pentecostal Holiness Church's parsonage. Some say she just didn't know what to do with this unnatural child that would suffer all the days of his life for her sinful ways. She didn't have a husband; she'd been going around with different men that lived at Mrs. Sadie's Boarding House for miners over in Beckley. Some say she just couldn't forgive herself, and she didn't have a hint at who the daddy was, so she wrapped poor Shorty in his blanket and put him in a paste board box on the preacher's porch. Nobody knowed her name and I guess they never will since she ran away with one of them men and ain't been heard from since. Our preacher's daddy, Reverend Otis Cox was the preacher of our church then, and him and Mrs. Molly took Shorty in. They gave him the last name of Moses, cause it reminded them of the story in the Bible. They raised him just like one of their own younguns and there ain't no better fellow anywhere in this world.

Mama says that when Shorty was a boy, that everybody thought that he would just stay around home, work the mines, play his guitar and sing for folks. Nobody ever thought that he would grow up, well up to three feet eleven inches, and find himself a wife. And she's normal, too. Well, she's normal in height and a little over normal in weight, but she's not hard to look at, least that's what folks say about her. Alice Marie Moses comes from a town call Floyd, Virginia, where she was teaching Sunday School in a little Holiness Church where Reverend Cox took Shorty and went there to hold revival. The revival went on for two whole weeks, the way it does when the spirit comes down and people are getting saved and sanctified and filled with the Holy Ghost, and at the end of those two weeks, Shorty asked Miss Alice to marry him. He had been saving his paychecks from the mine, he was still staying with the Cox's, but when he got back from Floyd, Virginia he bought a few acres of land from Gabrial Foster, just above the store in Logan's cove. Everybody around liked Shorty a bunch and was so happy for him finding a bride, that they all jumped right in and help build them a log cabin on his land. They had a big wedding at Glade Springs Pentecostal Holiness Church, too. Just about everybody in the community came. Some say a lot was there cause they was just curious as to how it would look, a midget marrying a big woman, but everybody that came brought a present, like is the custom, so Shorty and Miss Alice ended up setting up housekeeping with a lot of brand new stuff.

They have been married now for about ten years, and they have four young'uns themselves. Folks around here couldn't wait to see how that first one would turn out. Pap says there was even bets made amongst the menfolk as to whether or not it would be a midget. It was, a little bitty boy midget just like Shorty was when he was found on the porch of the Pentecostal Holiness Church parsonage. Then there was two more young'uns born, another boy and a girl, and they was both as normal as could be. Then about two years ago, another girl was born and she's a midget, too. So, I guess that about evens everything out, and Shorty's bunch seems to be one of the happiest in the whole south of West Virginia.

Chapter Sixteen

When we got back down to Gabe's store, we stopped to pick up Marsha and all the members of the Dees clan. If you went straight across the road here instead of turning left to go to Glade Springs, you'd pass by the farm that belongs to Uncle Dallas, Pap's youngest brother. He owns land on both sides of the road plum on down into Raleigh County and he grows burley tobacco. The Dees work for Uncle Dallas and live on the farm cause Uncle Dallas and Auntie Lil don't have no family of their own to do the work. They did have one son, his name was Joseph, but he was killed when their brand new Farmall tractor turned over on him when he was breaking land about ten years back. All the farmers around here has always used mules to plow with, but Uncle Dallas had made enough money on his farm and he bought him a tractor. His reasoning was that he wanted to plow up a lot more land but he wasn't thinking about how steep them hills was in some of his fields. Joseph had took the tractor up on the terrace, and the further up he plowed the steeper it got. Nobody ever thought about that tractor turning over, but when Joseph didn't come back to the house and it had got dark, Uncle Dallas went out to look for him. And there he found him mashed dead under it. I heard tell that the motor was still running when Uncle Dallas got there. They was so upset about it that they let that new Farmall tractor set under a shed for almost five years before it was ever used again. Joseph's grave is in a little fence just back of their house and flowers that Auntie Lil's planted on it bloom out every year in the spring.

The Dees are the only colored folks that lives near us in the Greenbriar River Valley, so they go to the same school as us. Mr. Ollie Dees and his wife Carolina, their six younguns and thirteen grand younguns live in two four room houses on the farm about a quarter mile from the crossroads. They have boys and girls from first grade on up to the tenth that goes to school and they walk up to Gabe's store to catch the bus. A grown up, sometimes old Mr. Dees himself, always walks to the bus stop with them cause there's been trouble between them and the Whitts, arguing and fighting and such. The Whitts calls them niggers and tells them that they stink and that they oughta go back down south and work on a plantation picking cotton where they belong. When they go at it, it scares the little ones and James, Mr. Dees oldest grandson, has fought with Kenneth Whitt more than once over it. I ask Mama one time what a nigger was, and she told me it was ugly and mean and that if she ever heard any of her young'uns call the Dees niggers that she would smack us right in the mouth. She said that the Whitts was jealous cause the Dees were more decent folks than they was, and they knowed how to raise tobacco and weren't afraid of work. As a matter of fact, Uncle Dallas says they was the best help he's ever had. And Gram always did say that them Dees young'uns was the best behaved young'uns in the valley. And I know why, too. I saw him one time when me and Pap was helping Uncle Dallas in his tobacco, when he was mad at them young'uns. He had a big long switch and them young'uns in a circle and him in the middle, and while they walked around him he was switching everyone of them good. So, they was nice and minded most of the time, never talking much except to each other, and they was right smart in school too. Annette Dees sits behind Barbara Anne in Mrs. Stones fifth grade class, and Barbara Anne says she almost always has all the right answers. I don't know why the Whitts say they stink neither cause most the time they smell like cinnamon and apples. Miss Dees cooks up a lot of cider from the apples that grow in Uncle Dallas' orchard, and she makes the best apple butter in the county. She wins the blue ribbon for her cider and apple butter just about every year when we have the county fair. I don't know of any ribbons the Whits has ever won for anything.

Chapter Seventeen

All the Dees young uns always look neat and clean when they come to school, too. I guess Uncle Dallas pays the Dees' right good every fall when he sells his tobacco cause they start school with nice clothes and new pencils. And I know you can make good money in tobacco, Uncle Dallas paid me ten whole dollars one year when I had helped him. I was about ten years old then and me and Pap would go over and spend the night at the tobacco barns so we could keep the fires going. Uncle Dallas raises flue-cured tobacco. The barns have great big stove pipes running through them coming from a big fireplace on the outside, and the heat from the fire goes through the pipes and heats up the barn real hot so that the tobacco would dry out. The men all go out to the fields and cut down the stalks of ripe green tobacco and put them in sleds with runners built on them so they'll slide easy behind the mule when he pulls it, and bring them to the barn. Then they'd put about five stalks on a stick and hang it on the tier poles in the barn. You had to be careful how you hung the sticks. They have to be put on the poles real even so the heat can get up through them all the same. It takes about a week to cure a barn of tobacco, and somebody had to keep the fires burning until it's all dried out right.

That's one time that folks all talked about how hard Pap did work and they told how much he'd helped out Uncle Dallas. Uncle Dallas had a bout with appendicitis and had to have a operation so it was too much for him to put the wood on the fire, and Mr. Dees and his crowd worked all day long and couldn't stay up all night too. Well, Pap did keep wood on the fires, but to be honest it wasn't all the reason he was there. Pap had this passion for coon hunting, and Gram fussed at him when he went too much, mainly cause he would drink shine while he was about it, but he could set out at the barns and listen to the dogs run and still keep the fires going. And, if they treed nearby, he'd go shake down the coon for them and get back in time to build up the fires again. I'll have to admit that I got a feeling when I heard them dogs run, too. I loved Uncle Dallas' old hound dogs, he gave me the two I have at my place now, and me and Pap had a good time that summer laying out in the back of that old truck on them old bed springs that he had put in there with a quilt over it, listening to them dogs run.

Some nights when we was tending the fires, Mr. Dees would come out to the barn, if he wasn't too tired from working in the fields all day. And sometimes he brought his fiddle with him and while we sat there in the dark he played it. Course I already knowd that Mr. Dees liked playing his fiddle at night. Cause not too long after they moved on to Uncle Dallas' farm, folks started telling tales about hearing some wild animal in the woods after dark. Pap said that there'd always been scary stories told here in the mountains about critters they called the "demon creatures". They say that men hunting on the mountain had seen it, and that it was big and black and when it stood up it was over seven feet tall. And it had a long tail that was real bushy, little bitty eyes that glowed as red and hot looking as fire and a long nose with big sharp teeth. They say that you can smell it long afore you'd see it and that if hunting dogs was to come up on it that they would turn tail and run. Now these folks was convinced that the noises that they heard was the "demon creature" wondering through the hills screeching and screaming and aiming to catch him somebody to eat. And they'd probably still be telling that tale, too, if Uncle Dallas hadn't heard some of them talking about the "demon creature' down at the General Store. When they told where it was that they heard it, then Uncle Dallas put their minds to rest by telling them that that was Mr. Dees setting out at night under the stars playing his fiddle.

Those songs he played at the barn would stand my hair up on my head. It seemed like they was all real slow and sad, not like the ones he played when we was at the Glade Springs Annual Picnic. Why, at the picnic, he would be sawing on that fiddle fast as lightning and his right foot would be going to town keeping in time with his fiddling. But the ones he played at the barn were soulful like. I can remember thinking that sometime I wanted to ask Mr. Dees about them songs, about why they sounded so sad and all, like maybe he was trying to tell some sad story with his fiddle and bow. Well, if I remember it, I'll ask him the next time we go to the picnic.

We really didn't work too hard them nights at the barns, but we did work pretty hard onced the tobacco was cured and ready to tie up to take to market. The cured tobacco was got down out of the barn and moved to the pack house. That's where it had to be got in order. Then it had to be stripped from the stalks and tied in bundles. Every bundle has to be about the same size, maybe about ten leaves at one time all put straight with the stems even. Then a tie leaf was used to wrap around the end of the stems to hold them together and then the end of that leaf was tucked between the leaves so it wouldn't come loose and fall off. It looked real neat like this and it made it easier to pack. Then it was put in piles on a flat tobacco basket with the pretty tied stems lay-ing to the outside, and then tied up with a burlap tobacco sheet so it would stay in order till it was sold at Marsh's Warehouse over in Wheeling. I was happy to get my ten dollars that year and I did have fun listening to Mr. Dees play his fiddle and hearing the dogs run at night, but I was allergic to the to-bacco dust and cause it gave me such a headache, Mama wouldn't let me work the next summer. She said it was better for me to stay home out of the pack house cause it made me sick, and besides it was making a tom-boy out of me.

Chapter eighteen

After Marsha Foster and the Dees' gets on the bus, William Earl turns left again going towards Glade Springs. It's just a little ways down Highway 19 before we have to turn left again and go back up on the mountain. You can see the turn from Gabe's Store. This road's called Watts Hollow and it's the last time we have to go up the mountain before getting into Glade Springs. Right up near the top of Watts Hollow was where Pap came courting Gram near to fifty years ago. Gram's mama and daddy was Howell and Hattie Watts and some member of their family has lived here on this mountain ever since it was still a part of Virginia. Pap and Gram had knowed each other all their lives, the Coles and The Watts has been members of the Pentecostal Holiness Church for as long as anybody can remember. Gram said she'd always knowed that she would marry Henry Lewis Cole ever since she was a youngoun, she just didn't think it would be quite so soon as it was. Henry and Dallas, Pap's brother, used to come up to the Watts' place with their mama and daddy when they was just boys, then when Pap got to be about fifteen or so, he just couldn't stay out of that hollow. Gram said he come up there so much that their old grey work horse that he rode would just come up that mountain natural, like he was trained to it.

Gram said that most of the time when they'd come, they'd all play silly games like hide and seek, so her mam and pap would think that they was still thinking like youngouns, but it was really so they could get where nobody could see them, then he'd kiss her. Gram was just thirteen then, the same age as me, but she said she knowd then that she loved the handsome dude. Well it didn't take too long for Gram's mama and daddy to figure out what was really going on out in that hay loft and they run Pap off for a while. But he just kept sneaking back up that hollow and Gram kept sneaking out of the house to meet with him, so when Pap was sixteen and Gram just turned fourteen, they was married at the Glade Springs Pentecostal Holiness Church.

Once when I was talking with Gram, it was when I had first started getting my period, and she was telling me about babies and about what men and women did after they got married, I found out that Gram didn't even know what was going to happen to her on her wedding night. She told me her and Pap was riding in the buggy going up to Pap's place where they was going to stay with Pap's mama, his daddy had died by then, and they seen two dogs doing it. Gram said Pap started grinning real big and told her that's what they was going to do. She said she thought he was just funning until when they got back to the house and got in bed that night and he got on top of her and started trying to hump. She said she was so mad that she dumped Pap right out in the middle of the floor and told him he wasn't going to treat her like any old dog. It went on like this for a few days and then Pap finally put aside his embarrassment and told his mama so she could talk to Gram. Well, I reckon it must have all worked itself out, cause the two of them had nine younguns and they've been married forty-eight years come this spring.

We didn't go all the way up to Gram's home place with the bus, there ain't any younguns that lives up there now, just Gram's brother George and he's a widower and none of his younguns cept one, his daughter, lives close by. We turn around in Jacob Wood's driveway.

There ain't no youngouns on the Wood property either. As a matter of fact there ain't even no house there anymore. Aaron Jacob Wood bought that land, across the road from Aunt Dorothy, from Gram and Pap and built a great big fine house for his bride, Monika Renate Andes. Jacob brought Monika back with him when he came home from fighting the Nazis' in Germany. He found her over there and just couldn't live without her even though folks said she was just looking for a way to get to the good ol United States and besides, she was young enough to be his daughter. All his friends just knew it wasn't going to last but Jacob just told them to mind their own business. So, everybody just sat back and watched and waited to see what was gonna happen.

Monika Renate Andes Wood was so pretty and she liked to dress up in fancy clothes and show off in front of everybody. And Jacob, he just kept buying her dresses and shoes and lots of jewelry so she always looked like she was going off to a party somewhere, and I think that is just what happened.

It seems like Gram told me that they had been married for about four years when Monika started going over to Charleston to a night club there. I'm not really sure what a night club is but I guess it's a place that opens just at night and it must be sorta like the Masonic Lodge in Beckley cause it was told that Jacob caught Monika dancing real close with a man from Charleston. Jacob had bought Monika a brand-new Oldsmobile Special 90 series sedan and she had started driving all over even going as far as Charleston in it. Monika had told Jacob that she was going out with some girl friends that she had met since she came here from Germany and he was so crazy about her and wanted to please her so much, that he told her she could go where ever she wanted in her new car. This had been going on for several months when Monika didn't come home one night, she stayed in Charleston for a whole week end. I reckon then Jacob started having second thoughts about her going up to the state capitol and tried to keep her from going. Well, Monika just went on anyway and when Jacob went looking for her, he found her in the arms of another man dancing in the night club. I heard that he begged her to come back to Glade Springs with him, but now she wanted to stay there with her friends.

Jacob came on back by himself and nobody really knowd what and all he went through, but the man just went slap crazy. The say he stayed in that big old house and didn't come out for weeks, not even when Monika came and got all her beautiful things and packed them in her Oldsmobile. People said he didn't ever turn no lights on in the house, just set there in the dark, so when Jacob set the house afire everybody anywhere on this side of Glade Springs saw the glow coming from the house and knowd something was wrong. Sheriff Barnes and all the firemen from the Big Walker Mountain Volunteer Fire Department was there in just a few minutes and tried to put the fire out.

Now the fire station ain't very far from Jacob's house, it's right near the Glade Springs city limits sign, and it didn't take too long before all the men had their equipment and the fire truck up to the house. But even though the firemen had the 1930 Ahrens Fox Quad fire truck with its 100-gallon tank, and they all worked real hard, they could not put out that fire before that big old house had done burnt to the ground. All that was left was them two big chimneys.

At first ever body thought that Jacob Wood was in the house when it burnt, but Sheriff Barnes saw him walking around and around at the back of his property. When the sheriff went up to Jacob and tried to talk to him, Jacob didn't even know who Sheriff Barnes was. The story told was that the sheriff had to take poor ol' Jacob way up to Weston, West Virginia and they put him in the Trans Alleghany Lunatic Asylum. I guess he is still there, nobody ever talks about him anymore. And nobody has seen hide nor hair of Monika Wood. I reckon she's still over in Charleston with her friends.

Chapter nineteen

After we turn around in the Wood driveway, we stop in front of Aunt Dorothy's house. Aunt Dorothy is Gram's oldest sister and the sweetest person that the Good Lord ever put on this earth. She is one of those folks that you can look at in her face and tell that she's been born again: saved, sanctified and filled with the Holy Ghost. And she's been this way just about all her whole life. Gram says that when they was youngouns and they'd go out to play, that Aunt Dorothy always wanted to play church. She'd take her younger brothers and sisters down to the woods, preach to them for a while and then baptize them all in the creek. Gram said she'd been baptized so many times that she was bound to go to heaven. But Aunt Dorothy wasn't the preaching kind that gets on your nerves or makes you mad. She has a way about her that makes you love her and want to do good when you are around her.

And she ain't never done nobody no wrong, even though there was a plenty done to her. Her husband Edward was real mean to her, always calling her names and making fun of her praying and trying to help people. Gram said that one time Aunt Dorothy was praying about a heavy burden she was carrying and he kept yelling at her to stop. So Aunt Dorothy went to the outhouse to pray. Well, Edward was so mad that she didn't stop praying that he went out there and threatened to turn the outhouse over if she didn't come out. But she never would say no harm against him, even when she found out that he had a woman on the other side of Beckley that he had been treating just like a wife for years. He even had some young'uns with her. Aunt Dorothy just prayed through that too and kept on going in her sweet gentle way same as she always had before. They didn't have any young'uns themselves and folks said that she should have kicked him down that mountain and went on with her life, but Aunt Dorothy didn't believe in divorce, and she believed that ever thing that happened was God's will, and was done for a purpose, and it was her plot in life to bear whatever God gave her to bear.

I don't know not one other soul on this earth that would have took all this meanness and still be nice about it. But Aunt Dorothy did. She even ended up raising two of them three young'uns just like her very own when Edward and their mama and the other one was killed in that house fire. Folks who saw it said that house went up just like a tinder box, once it got started it couldn't a been stopped even if they'd had a fire house next door. Folk say that it burnt faster than Jacob Wood's did years later. It seems like, from what people told, that Aunt Dorothy's husband, that woman and them younguns was all asleep upstairs in that old house they'd rented out on Highway 41 just east of Beckley when it caught fire. There ain't nobody who really knows just what all happened, but it seems that they couldn't get anybody out but them two little girls, and they was just babies then, so they can't remember anything either. Anyhow, Aunt Dorothy did her Christian duty and took them two right in her house. She even said that Edward and that woman and young un could be buried in the Watt's family plot at Glade Springs Pentecostal Holiness Church, but this was one time that Gram had put her foot down hard. She said that she'd had to put up with that sorry, low down and good for nothing man ever since he'd married Aunt Dorothy, but she'd just be durn if she'd spend eternity laying beside him in the family plot no matter how much shamming folks did. She didn't even feel one bit guilty when they had to be buried in Potter's field between Glade Springs and Beckley. Course, she did say later that she'd have changed her mind about the youngoun if folks had kept on at her. And she always treated them other two youngouns good after Aunt Dorothy took them in.

Most of the neighbors say there had to have been some bad blood there somewhere, probably on Edwards side, cause even with all that they had a good Christian raising, both of them girls went bad. The oldest one named Carolyn left and ain't nobody heard from her since. Edna Lee run off for awhile then she showed back up at Aunt Dorothy's with two youngouns of her own. Of course Aunt Dorothy with her forgiving nature took her back in just like she ain't never left and done wrong. Gram said that Edna Lee stayed all of three months and then she took off again and left them little ones there for Aunt Dorothy to see to, and she's had them ever since. That's who we pick up first when we go up Watts Hollow. Mary Ellen and Catherine. Mary Ellen is twelve years old and Catherine is eleven. I'm not sure just what they have been told about their mama and daddy, but I know they call Aunt Dorothy, Grandma, and they act like they love her just like I love Gram. They're both real sweet little girls, pretty too, and me and my sisters, I'm the only one so far who knows the real story about them, claim them to be our cousins, and we like them enough that if you'd say anything bad to them, we'd like as not be ready to fight.

Chapter twenty

Our sheriff here in Fayette County is Howard Glenn Barnes, and him and his wife Priscilla live right near the bottom of Watts Hollow. Most folks around here say that Sheriff Barnes is the best sheriff that we've had in a long time, course he's the only one I've ever knowed since he's been sheriff ever since I've been born. I don't see him much, usually just at the Glade Springs annual picnic, and when he leads off the Christmas parade in his patrol car with the red light, that sets on the hood flashing, and he'll blow the siren. This year he was in his brand new black and white that he had just got, looking all proud. Pap says he don't see why he couldn't have drove the old car just one more time since the new one still had a shield with "Richmond Police Patrol" in gold letters on both sides. They had got the 1941 Ford from the Richmond, Virginia Police Department when they had bought new 1945 sedans and put their old cars up at auction. Seems like the sheriff would've waited until he got the letters changed, but I guess he was too ashamed for everybody to see the old patrol car as beat up as it was after he had chased them three excaped convicts from the Bluefield Penal Farm all over the county then hit that patch of ice in the road and landed stuck in snow when he went down that steep bank out on Highway 19 east of town. Sheriff Barnes didn't get hurt bad, just some sore bones I heard, cause the snow had softened the blow, but the patrol car was pretty much banged up. He did drive it back to town though, after Mr. John

Ayers and his boys, who live just this side of the Greenbriar County line, hooked up a team of mules to it and pull it back up on the road. He parked it behind the jail when he got it back and then went over to Richmond and got the new one. Pap says they'll probably end up fixing up the old patrol car for Deputy Ben Hicks to drive since he ain't never had one of his own.

Folks say that Fayette County is a good place to live cause there ain't very much trouble that goes on here, but if you ever do need him, you can almost always find Sheriff Barnes down at his jail where him and Deputy Ben Walker and Millicent Ross, that's William and Albert Paul's mama, works. Sheriff Barnes got Millicent to come to work when they got in their new radio. Now she can call out, if somebody needs the sheriff or Ben, right to the car. That's how Sheriff Barnes came to be chasing them excape convicts. The sheriff from over in Greenbriar County had called the jail and told Millicent that they was in Fayette County, and she had called out to Sheriff Barnes, and he took off after them when he saw them in that car they had stole out on Highway 41. Course he never did catch them convicts, but he did turn them back towards Bluefield. I think that's what he's more ashamed of than that the patrol car got tore up.

The new patrol car has a two-way radio in it, the old one had one where Millicent could talk to Sheriff Barnes and Ben, but they couldn't talk back. With the two-way radio that they have now, the sheriff and Ben can talk to her, too, when she calls them. Now, I guess it's a good thing that they got the new car when they did cause it was just two days after Christmas when that two way radio came in real handy. Coleman Whitt, who lives out Highway 19 west of town had got drunk on moonshine and was beating up on his wife Bonnie. One of the Whitt youngouns had gone over to Gabe's Store and called the jail and told Millicent that Sheriff Brown needed to come get Coleman and lock him up til he got sober. So the sheriff went all the way out to the Whitts with the red light flashing and the siren going, the first time in a while that he had to use them for something else besides the parade, to try to get it all straightened out. They live about a half mile off the main highway down a dirt road, and they was still going at it when the sheriff got there. Well, it seems like Coleman Whitt put up quite a fight when the sheriff tried to get him to get in the car, cause Sheriff Barnes had to put handcuffs on him and was carrying him to the patrol car with one hand on the back of his collar and one hooked in his belt, when Bonnie Whitt came out of the house yelling at the sheriff to leave her husband alone. She jumped up on his back and was hitting him with her fist. I can just imagine what that looked like cause the sheriff ain't no little man, Gram says he'll dress out at about three hundred pounds, and Bonnie Whitt probably don't weigh a hundred pounds soaking wet. Then the Whitt youngouns got in on it, they was running around like wild Indians and throwing apples and tangerines. They was hitting their mama, too, and she just kept getting madder and madder and beating harder on Sheriff Barnes. Then it seems like the sheriff just didn't have much choice and had to let go of Coleman and get to the patrol car to call for help.

Mr. Ross had gone to the jail to pick up Millicent to take her home, and he was there when the sheriff called hollering over the radio for them to get Ben out there. He went and picked up Ben and they went as fast as they could in Mr. Ross' car out to Coleman Whitt's place. Mr. Ross told Pap that when him and Ben pulled up in the Whitt's yard, that Bonnie was riding Sheriff Barnes like he was a bucking bronco, kicking him in his sides just like she was spurring him along. The younguns ran and hid, still throwing apples and tangerines until they got plum out of sight, when they saw Ben and Mr. Ross drive up. Soon as he got out of the car, Ben ran over and tried to get Bonnie off of the sheriff's back and she turned on him, fighting like a wild cat and getting the best of him, too, cause he ain't much bigger that she is. Finally, the sheriff and Ben got her under control but not before they had to put handcuffs on her, too, to keep her from going after them again. Mr. Ross said that the sheriff and Ben just stood there looking around sorta stunned for a few minutes, then Sheriff Barnes told them to look after Coleman and Bonnie til he got back. He stayed gone about twenty minutes or so, and when he came back, he was followed by three trucks full of Whitts, and old man Caleb Whitt himself was driving the lead truck. They jumped out of them trucks almost before they was stopped good, grabbed up Coleman and Bonnie and took them in their house. The sheriff went in behind them and when he came out all he was carrying was them two sets of handcuffs. He got in his new patrol car and left and didn't say a word to nobody.

After they all got back to the jail, and Millicent had put methylate and band aids on their scratches and had looked after their bruises, Sheriff Barnes had a black eye that swelled almost plum shut where one of them Whitt younguns had hit him in the eye with an apple, Ben asked the sheriff how he got them other Whitts to come out and help him with Coleman and Bonnie. Mr. Ross said that the sheriff sat there with a big thick piece of steak on his eye, that he took home that night and had Priscilla cook up medium rare for him, and told them about going over to old man Whitt's place. He told them that Caleb said at first that Bonnie was Coleman's problem and he could do whatever he had to with her to keep her in line, and that it weren't none of their business how he handled his own wife. Then the sheriff told Caleb that it was his business to report any suspicions about moonshiners to the revenuers if he didn't get complete cooperation from them that he was suspicioning. Mr. Ross says you can guess the rest, old man Caleb got in his truck, went down to two more Whitt houses and got his boys and still made it to Coleman's house right behind the sheriff. Sheriff Barnes said, too, that it was just as well that he hadn't had to lock up them Whitts, cause if he had, there'd be tobacco juice all over his jail house.

Chapter twenty-one

You could always count on Sheriff Barnes to be around if you needed him, though. They say that when Joseph got mashed under Uncle Dallas' new Farmall tractor, that the sheriff went just as soon as he heard and was there to help Uncle Dallas dig him out. They couldn't move the tractor off of Joseph without hooking something to it to pull it over and Uncle Dallas had loaned out his work horses for the summer, cause he didn't need them no more since he had that tractor, to a fellow down in Raleigh County and there weren't no way they could get them back fast enough to do any good. Course, as it turned out, it wouldn't have mattered cause Dr. Smith said that Joseph was already dead when he got there and he came up with Sheriff Barnes. But they dug him out with shovels and Sheriff Barnes picked him up and put him in his patrol car, I don't know which one he had then, and drove all the way over to Bickley to the hospital there. They said that when the doctor over there told them what they already knowed, that Joseph was dead, that the sheriff picked him up and carried him in his arms, over to Lancaster's Funeral Service, that's about two city blocks from the hospital, and stayed there with him until they had him cleaned up and ready to take back home for the wake. Later, it was told that if it hadn't of been for Sheriff Barnes, that it ain't no telling what would've happened, cause Uncle Dallas and Auntie Lil was both plum out of their minds and would have probably took Joseph in the house and kept him there.

And the sheriff was a man that wouldn't put up with nobody being mean to somebody without no cause neither. Mr. Wilham Schmit has been living in Glade Springs ever since he was a little boy, and he's close to the same age as my mama and daddy is, and him and his folks lived upstairs and run the German Bakery there on Main Street. You couldn't hardly walk by that bakery without going in to buy something it smelt so good, and you could smell it clear up to three blocks away, and even further is there was a breeze. And the Schmits was good about offering you a taste, I think it was just to make your mouth water too bad not to buy more, and they always acted real friendly to everbody. But after we was at war with his old country, some boys, and some of them was Whitts, started writing mean stuff all over the bakery windows and they drawed them swastikas on the walls and on the sidewalk in front of their place. Mr. Schmit's daddy had done died by then, and he just had his mama living there with him when all this was going on, and I heard that she got too scared to even come down and help Mr. Schmit do the baking. And, when somebody busted out one of the big windows and threw a burning bag of rags soaked in kerosene through it, she had a heart attack or something, and I ain't seen her out since then.

Now Sheriff Barnes couldn't ever prove that the Whitt's was the ones who did it, and they weren't old enough to arrest, but he went out to Calebs and had him to call all his younguns and grand-younguns together. Ben Walker told Pap that the sheriff took off his belt, took his gun holster off of it, layed it on the hood of the patrol car and told Caleb that if him or his boys, the daddy's of them others, didn't take a strap to them younguns that he was gonna do it himself. Ben said that Sheriff Barnes was so mad that his face was red as a beet and that his whole big body was just a shaking when he talked. The Whitts didn't even argue, Ben said them daddy's took off their belts and ever one of them boys that had been anywhere near Schmit's Bakery was whipped just like they was a bunch of dogs. It was a long time afore you saw any Whitts back in town and I don't recall ever seeing them in the bakery.

Gram always says that Sheriff Barnes has a heart to fit his body. There was times when he'd had to go tell folks when their boys had been killed in the war. And, they say he would stay right there and cry with them and then do whatever needed doing as far as getting them boys back home and buried near their families. And he did it for everbody, it didn't matter who they was.

Even as mean as the Whitts was, when Caleb's youngest son Auther Ray was killed while fighting for his country, Sheriff Barnes was right there with them. When Mrs. Whitt found out that they was going to send him home on a train all the way from New York City, she plum had a kaniption fit. She started crying and telling them about how much Arthur Ray was scared of trains, cause one time when he was little, he had almost got hit by the engine of one of the Chesapeake and Ohio trains out on the trestle over New River where it made the loop. Arthur Ray was playing out in the middle of that trestle and that train came up on him so fast that he near about didn't make it to the end of the trestle, and, he weren't one of them that wasn't afraid to jump off in the river, and he'd had a natural fear of trains ever since. She didn't want her boy riding home on one. Well Arthur Ray did have to ride the train home, but he didn't have to it by himself. Sheriff Barnes took it on hisself to go all the way to New York and ride back with him, and he was right there all night through the wake, too. He even went with the Whitt family when they took poor old Arthur Ray up to the little plank church and buried him in the graveyard there. Someday, I'm gonna ask Sheriff Barnes if he saw any of them serpents while he was up there.

Chapter twenty-two

The next stop was the one I had been waiting for since I'd figured that I wouldn't be talking to Albert Paul while we was riding the bus. It was Gilbert Marshall's trailer park. My best friend, Rachel Louise Abbott, lives in one of the new trailers, well almost new, that Mr. Marshall had bought right after the war in 1944 and put on his land just outside of town. There was so many men coming to work in the coal mines after we was at peace with the world, that there weren't places enough for them to stay. Some stayed in the mining houses if they could just get by with a bedroom, but if they had a family, it was hard to find a place where they could all fit in to. Mr. Marshall started out just putting four trailer houses on his place, but it weren't long before he had put more out there. Now there are ten in all and folks are still looking for a place to live. I ain't been in none of them except Rachels, but she has been in some of the others and she says they are all just alike. Just big enough to turn around in, but they're split up so there's two or three beds separated by a wall so they had some privacy. Then there's a little kitchen and a sitting room together. There's a sink, a gas cook stove and a Frigidaire in everyone but none of them have a bathroom. So, Mr. Marshall built some outhouses and put them at about every other one. I thought that Rachel's little box trailer was just as cute as cute could be, and I even thought about maybe me and Albert Paul living in one after we got married.

Most of the folks living in the trailer park weren't from here. They'd come to work in the mines cause they was getting more coal out now than they ever had before. Pap said Fayette County had once set some kind of record for how much coal they brought up since the railroad had built the Loop Creek Branch off from the mainline of the Chesapeake and Ohio Railway to come around our mines. Before they'd put the loop in, most of the coal was got over in Kanawha County cause the railroad run right through there. Mining companies had bought up most of the land around here cause it weren't worth much for anything else and they built little mining towns all around. Mount Hope, between here and Charleston, was the biggest one near us. That whole town burnt down one time and they built it right back. It's real modern too. They even have a movie house and their streets are paved and they have electric lights that light up the whole town. But it's so crowded that any new folks that come here have to stay in other towns close by.

That's how Rachael and her mama and daddy came to be living in Glade Springs. They couldn't find a house anywhere nearer Mount Hope. But I sure am glad they did, cause me and Rachael hit it off the first time we met on the school bus two years ago. We was friends in a instant. Rebecca and Rachael, friends for ever, that's what we wrote in black paint over on the Chesapeake and Ohio railroad trestle. Her family came here from Cherry Point, North Carolina. Her and her mama had even lived there on the marine base of Camp Lejune while her daddy had been off fighting for his country. They was close to the Atlantic Ocean and Rachael used to wear a bathing suit and go out swimming in it, and she said that her and her girlfriends would lay on the sand on a blanket while all the sailors would walk around and look at them. She said she had to sneak out to do it cause her mama would have killed her if she'd knowd she was letting them men look at her half naked. Rachael told me that this one time when she spent the night with a girl named Brenda Lewis, Rachael's mama was in the hospital for something, that they snuck out and went down to the beach after dark. Brenda knew a marine named Billy and he had a friend, he was a marine too, who's name was George and they met them down there. She said they went behind a sand dune and sat down on a blanket that they'd spread out on the sand. Billy and Brenda went walking and left her and George there by themselves. She said he started kissing her and that he touched her on her bosom. Rachael said she was ready to get married right then and there, but then he started holding her too tight and touching her too rough and she got scared and made him stop. But she said she still thought about it though and wondered what it would have been like if she had let him do it. I thought it was just so exciting and romantic and I always feel kinda funny, tickling like in my stomach, when we'd talk about it. It's the same way I'd felt that time when Albert Paul kissed me on my mouth.

Rachel's mama's real Christian like, and it was only cause me and my family went to Glade Springs Pentecostal Holiness Church, that she let me and Rachel be friends. They had started going to church with us when they first moved here. Well, her and Rachel went. Mr. Abbott didn't ever go and Rachel had told me that he went over to the tavern's in Mount Hope ever Sunday to drink beer. It was something to do with his being in the war, and him only having one hand, Rachel said he got the other one blowed off by a mine, the kind they used to blow up stuff in the army. She said she thought that he wouldn't go to church cause he was mad at God for letting him get crippled up. I really don't know what he was so mad about cause he seemed to be able to do most anything that he wanted to. He worked every day at the mine and he drove their car and worked around their house fixing things up, and he could tote anything, no matter how heavy it was once in got it tucked up under that arm.

He wasn't much of a friendly man, either. You hardly ever saw him out with Rachel and her mama up town or at the picnics and all. Most of the times when I was over at their place, he'd be in a chair beside the radio and sometimes he'd be snoring. This one time when I went home with Rachael after church, Mr. Abbott was fast asleep and he was holding a can of beer in his hand. Mrs. Abbott went and jerked it right out of his hand and poured that beer out down the sink. She was telling him the whole time what a shame and disgrace it was and that she was not going to have anybody drinking the devil's drink in her house, especially on the Lord's Day. Well, Mr. Abbott just got up and walked out the door and didn't say not one word back to her. He didn't come home neither for two or three days, not until Mrs. Abbott and Preacher Cox went over and found him in Mount Hope and talked him in to it. I guess her ranting got her her way, though, cause now Rachael says that he don't bring no beer in the trailer, that when he's drinking, he sits in his car over behind the Ice Plant down near the river and gets just as drunk as he wants to.

Its really bad that Mr. Abbott is the way he is now, cause I've seen a picture of him with his marine uniform on and he was so handsome. And they have some pictures that they made before he went in the service and he was hugging Mrs. Abbott and Rachael and just a grinning like he was so happy he didn't know what to do. Gram says that if Mr. Abbott would make peace with God that he'd stop all that drinking cause then he wouldn't be so miserable. She says that it's really himself that he's mad at cause he ain't man enough to accept the Lord's will about losing his hand. I sure hope he does make his peace with God. It would surely be nice to see him smiling and all like he was doing in them pictures.

Now, I'm just a little bit scared of Mrs. Abbott. I ain't scared that she'll hurt me none, just that maybe she'll stop me and Rachael from being friends. So I always act real proper when I'm around her. She's nice to me and invites me to go shopping and to church with them. But she won't let Rachael go to the movies or to the dances over at the Masonic Lodge. She believes it]s a sin. My mama feels a lot like that herself. She ain't never let us go to the movie theater over in Mount Hope and the only time we ever went to the Lodge dance was when Daddy was home one Saturday night and he took us. That was the night I saw them Barnette twins dance. I couldn't believe that we was actually going to go to a dance but Gram said she wasn't surprised, that my daddy could always talk Mama in to doing anything whether it was right or wrong. Well, I didn't talk about going to movies or dances or boys around Mrs. Abbott caused I knowed she was so much against it and I guess cause I never said anything, that she thought I was alright for Rachael to be around. The only time that she ever said anything at all against us being friends, was that time when we got took to the principal's office for looking at those naked pictures in the encyclopedia. But I know for a sure fact, that if she ever slips in on me and Rachael when we don't know she's around, and she hears us talking about marines and touching and dancing and kissing and what it's like to be married, that she'll probably change her mind about me.

I think Rachel is the prettiest girl in school, well ever since Sarah Jane Dillon stopped coming that is, I still think Sara Jane is the prettiest girl I've ever seen anywhere around here. But Rachael would be even prettier if her mama would let her wear clothes like mine. She makes Rachael dark colored, black or brown mostly, dresses and long skirts and long sleeve blouses that hang loose as a house dress on her. Why, Mrs. Abbott would have beat Rachael half to death if she'd wore a sweater clinging to her like my new pink Christmas sweater does. But Rachael loves pretty clothes and because she's my best friend, sometimes I let her borrow some of mine. It works out pretty good in the winter time cause she can put her coat on over anything that she don't want her mama to see, but in warm weather, I have to sneak things to her and she'll wait until we get away from her mama and then she'll change. Now don't get me wrong, my clothes are all proper to wear, but my mama will make ours with some style and color, like she has hemmed our skirts up a lot higher since the new fashion patterns show them like that.

Sometimes I feel a little guilty cause I'm helping Rachael go against her mama's wishes, but it sure don't seem to bother Rachael none. She says that someday she's going back to live down near Cherry Point, North Carolina, and she's gonna wear a bathing suit and lay on the beach all she wants to. And she says that she is gonna find her a marine to marry. But she don't want one that's gonna go off to war cause when they go away that way they ain't the same person when they get back. I know she's thinking about her daddy when she talks like that. She says her husband is gonna be tall and handsome, and fun and he will take her to all the dances there is on the base and when he gets his transfers, that they will travel all over the world together. But first, soon as she turns eighteen years old, she wants to go to Hollywood, California.

I feel partly to blame about Rachael wanting so bad to go to California, because I'm the one that's been telling her all about it. Now I don't know when I learned to read, it seems like I've just been doing it all my life and I read all the time I can. And, I love reading in magazines best of all, cause they have the pictures to go along with the words, and you can see what things really are like and you don't have to imagine so hard. I would read to Rachael and show her all the pages about what was going on out in Hollywood. Life Magazine would have a full colored picture on their cover ever few months of one of the movie stars like Greta Garbo and Betty Grable, and half the time they was wearing clothes that showed off their busoms and their legs. On this one cover Betty Grable just had on what looked like her brazier and drawers, but it was one of them two piece bathing suits. And they always looked so pretty and there was always some good looking movie star in love with them. You could tell it by the way they would look into each others eyes. And if they didn't like them anymore after they got married to them, they'd just get a divorce, and get another one. In one of the magazines about Greta Garbo, it told how she had already been married three times to different men. And it's something else how everbody just about worships these movie stars. This is just what Rachael thinks she wants out of life, everybody making over her and different men falling in love with her all the time. Not me though. All I want is to be a teacher just like Miss Covington and have Albert Paul Ross to come begging at my feet like them women said their men did when they got hold to Miss Claire's potion.

Chapter twenty-three

When we pick up Rachael and the other younguns that live in the trailer park, they're all real little and I don't know nothing about them, we just have to go about three quarters of a mile down the road until we pass by the Glade Springs City limits sign. Right across the line on the left hand side is the flour mill and ice plant that is run by Ezra Osborne and his wife Edna. And they have their house built right on to the side of the mill so it makes it easy for them to get back and forth to work. She's the one that can make the best lemon aid and home made ice cream in the world that she brings to the annual picnics. And we love going to the ice plant on real hot days, cause Mr. Osborne has this machine that can shave a block of ice and make it fine like snow. He'll put some in a paper that he rolls up and bends on the end, so the ice won't fall out, and we eat it, and there ain't nothing no better when the sweats pouring off you than to have some of that store made snow to put in your mouth, unless you have enough money to buy a RC Cola. Mrs. Osborne puts them RC's in a number two wash tub and packs ice chunks all around them, and when you get them out and open them by that opener with RC Cola wrote on it, that Mr. Osborne has nailed up right there at the door, sometimes they'll have ice right in the cola. That's just about being plum near to heaven. Mama don't let us have too many of those RCs, though. She says that milk is better for your skin and bones, and besides, we can get all the milk we want for free. Them

RCs cost money and if you don't drink them there, you have to pay a deposit on the bottle, too. Mr. Osborne told us that if we pick up empty RC bottles that folks throw out beside the road, that he'll give us two cents for ever one we find and then when we get enough, we can buy our own RC's.

Mr. Osborne is a real nice fellow. We used to see him more back during the war, though. He was the Fayette County, West Virginia Air Raid Warden and he worked for the National Civil Air Patrol. He used to go around everbody's houses wearing his white helmet and carrying his flashlight and showing us pictures of them Japanese and German airplanes so we'd know what they looked like if they ever got over on our peaceful shores. And he'd check to make sure we all had our black window shades so we could pull them down at night so them Japanese couldn't make out our houses in the dark if they did get over here. He gave me and Barbara Ann a badge with Civil Air Patrol on it and a little bag that we could carry over our shoulder with a flashlight and a first aid kit in it, cause we knew which airplanes was ours and which ones was the enemies. And it wasn't all that easy neither, cause he didn't show us airplanes with swastikas and circles on them. What he show us was called silhouettes, just black shapes of airplanes, so you had to know how all them airplanes was different and not by what was painted on them. Course I'm too old now to be wearing a pretend badge even if it does have National Civil Air Patrol on it, but Barbara Ann pinned hers on her winter coat, and I reckon if that coat would still fit her, she'd still be wearing that badge.

Chapter twenty-four

Just across the road from Mr. Osborne's is Tyson's General Store. It was built from brick and has a porch all the way across the front of it. And in great big letters up over the porch it says, "Tyson's General Store". Pete Collins works for Mr. Tyson, and every morning bright and early you can see him moving stuff out to the porch. It's mostly hardware, like shovels, chicken wire and such. He puts it out there real neat so when folks come looking for something, they can find it without no trouble. It's a big store, bigger even than the company store over at Price Hill Junction, and you can get most of what you'd ever need right here in the town of Glade Springs. There ain't no need to go all the way to Beckley or Charleston for anything, unless you just wanted to ride that far, cause if Mr. Tyson don't already have it in his store, then he'll order it for you and it'll be here in just a few days.

I never would linger much out on the porch. First, cause there ain't nothing out there that I want, and I don't like the way that Pete Collins is always looking at me. Maybe he's just trying to be friendly, but I don't feel real friendly towards him. Now, he ain't never done nothing wrong in front of me, but it feels like something that I don't like is crawling on me evertime he acts like he's got to hand me something and his fingers touch me on my hand. Mary Beth says its cooties. She swore she'd give me her Nancy Ann Story Book Princess doll if she weren't telling the truth when she said that she'd seen some run down the back of his neck one day when he sat down on the steps of the store and took his cap off. I wouldn't wonder that he has some bugs of some kind on him, cause I don't think he ever changes clothes. He always has on them yellow looking hunting pants that keep falling down and showing his crack cause he's skinny as a bean pole and don't have no hips to hold his pants up with. And he wears that same old ragged green shirt. I don't think he's poor though, cause he lives in one of them new trailers over in Marshall's Trailer Park, and he works everday for Mr. Tyson.

I don't know much about Pete, and I can't even tell how old he is neither. He don't look no older than William Earl, but he's always hanging around with Samuel Logan and Dewey McFarland, and both of them is bout near the same age as Daddy. Rachael says that she ain't never seen nobody at his trailer except for Samuel and Dewey and Mr. Tyson when he comes to pick him up for work if it's raining real hard or it's really cold. She said she walked by his place one day last summer, when he had his door standing wide open cause it was hot, and when she looked in, she didn't see nothing except a mason jar setting beside a pallet on the floor. I know he ain't from here, though, cause I've heard that much, and, he talks like a Yankee. Rachael says she thinks he was in the Navy cause when he rolls up the sleeves on that old green shirt, you can see tattoos on his arms, and, she says that just about all sailors get them tattoos. Gram, who suspicions everbody, says she thinks he's hiding from the law. That he was probably in the pen somewhere up north and broke out. Aunt Dorothy heard Gram say that, and she said maybe he had served some time and paid his debt to society, then came down here to get a new start. She said that we needed to be nice to him and make him feel welcome. Well, I don't care where he comes from, and I really don't even care about his cooties except he better not let one of them get off on me.

Chapter twenty-five

On the same side of the street with Tyson's General Store is the First Bank and Trust Company, Lawyer Warren T. Barker's office, Schmit's Bakery and Marshall's Furniture Store. All of these are joined together to make one big long building, but they're separated on the insides and you have to go in them by their own doors. The First Bank and Trust Company is first. It belongs to John Randall Nichols II, and when you go in, there's a big picture of John Randall Nichols, Founder, and the daddy of John Randall Nichols II, hanging so everbody has to look at it first thing. Now, I don't care about seeing none of these Nichols. You can tell by looking at all of them, even the picture of John Randall Nichols, Founder, that there's nastiness running all through their veins. Pap says that they think that they're stuff don't stink cause they have all that money and ride around in a Chrysler. And, I can't stand that John Randall Nichols III. He always acts like he's better than everbody else, wearing his suit and white shirt to school just like he was going to church. He's a tattletale and a sissy, too. When Mr. Davis, our music director was getting the school band together, John Randall wanted to play the xylophone.

Daddy don't want me saying nothing bad about them though, he talks about Mr. Nichols likes he's one of his best friends, cause when Daddy wanted to buy his Mack truck, Mr. Nichols lent him the money. One time I heard him and Mama fussing about him being gone on the road so much, and he was telling her he had to stay out to pay for his truck right on time. He couldn't let Mr. Nichols down cause he had helped him out and he had to keep his trust. Mama said she didn't care about whether he let Mr. Nichols down or not, but that he'd better make them payments on time, cause they both knowed whos land it was that was mortgaged to get that truck. Well, I know that Daddy owns that truck out free and clear now, and I know something else, too. If he ever wants anything else from Mr. Nichols, that they better be friends, cause Mama ain't planning to mortgage her land again. She said the only reason Daddy likes Mr. Nichols so much for loaning him that money is cause it's a sure fired way to get to stay away.

Next door to the First Bank and Trust Company is Schmit's Bakery. I told you about the meanness that was done to the Schmits during the war, and folks wondered if they'd stay here after that. Well, they did. Mr. Schmit is still baking up all them good smelling rolls and pastries, and he got married about a year ago. His wife's name is Tillie. And she's real nice and friendly and, I'm not really sure, but I think she's from over in Germany, too. Now Mr. Schmit has somebody to help him again, since his mama still won't come down the stairs, and Tillie is right in there with him ever morning early as can be putting icing on them cakes and filling up them eclairs with cream. And, I heard over at Maxine's last time we was there, that Miss Tillie is going to have a baby. It's real sad about old Mrs. Schmit, though, we can see her looking down on the street from the window sometimes, but she won't wave at you even if you wave at her first.

Warren T. Barker, Attorney At Law is right next to Schmit's Bakery. Gram says he's as crooked as the day is long, but he seemed like a right nice fellow when he came to our school and spoke to our class on what it's like to live in Washington D.C., our nation's capital. He was a state representative for West Virginia and lived there and worked at the capitol building. He said it was partly his job to help make the laws that protect the people of these United States. He talked right favorably about Washington D.C. and his job, so I don't know why he came back here to Glade Springs to live. Maybe it's because he's old and can't work much no more. Pap says he was down to earth his whole life up until he went away to that fancy college up north to become a lawyer. Him and Mr. Barker used to roam these hills together hunting and exploring when they was boys and they'd talked about going to work in the mines together. They wanted to go down in the shafts to see what it was like that far down under the ground. But Pap said that Mr. Barker's folks were dead set against him working the coal mines, why, they'd never have got over the shame of it, the son of a lawyer, old Mr. Barker was a lawyer, too, going to work in the coal mines like common folks. They packed him up and sent him off to Harvard University just as soon as he finished all his eleven grades of school to become Mr. Warren T. Barker, Attorney at Law.

When he came back to West Virginia the first time after he'd been to Harvard University, him and his wife, he'd met her in Massachusetts, lived over in Charleston. I don't recall anybody saying anything about younguns, so I reckon it was just him and her. That's where he practiced being a lawyer and I reckon he got right good at it cause later he was voted to the United States House of Representatives by the good people of West Virginia. I don't know how long he's been back here in Glade Springs, but it must have been quite some time cause he's been around as long as I can remember. He lives in that big old house on Elm Street that he grew up in, his mama and daddy have both passed on, with just his wife. About the only time I've ever seen Mr. Barker, except when he came to our school, was at the annual picnic, cause they go to church at the First Presbyterian Church, right across the street from his office there on Main Street and they don't visit back and forth across the county like most folks. Pap says he sees him ever once in a while when he'll come out to Gabe's Store and they'll set out on the porch, or in around the stove if it's winter time, and talk about the way things was when they was growing up.

Chapter twenty-six

Marshall's Furniture Store is right next to Mr. Barker's office. This is the same Mr. Marshall that has the trailer park just outside of town where Rachael lives, and I love going in his store. My imagination can run wild as a jack rabbit when I'm in there looking at all that brand new furniture and planning just what mine and Albert Paul's house is gonna look like. I ain't never seen nothing no prettier than that red settee that Mr. Marshall has sitting on that rug right there as you come in the door. Mama says that rug came here all the way from Japan, I reckon we're not enemies with them no more, and it's called a oriental rug. Well, I want me one of them oriental rugs, whether we're enemies with Japan or not, and a red settee when I marry Albert Paul and set up housekeeping. And, I want that cherry poster bed with its matching chifforobe, and it's got this beautiful thick mattress and it's box springs is cover up just like the mattress so you can't even see them springs in it. One day when me and Rachael was in there, while Mama was paying on her new Frigidaire, I had Rachael keep watch and I climbed right up on that mattress and laid down like I was sleeping on it. And, I bet that I could've gone right on off to sleep, too, and dreamed of me and Albert Paul laying in this bed if I'd had a pillow and quilt.

When Rachael went with us to Marshall's Furniture Store, she usually spent most of the time watching the television set that he had. She'd tell me, course she wouldn't say it loud enough for my mama or hers who ever we was with to hear, that we was gonna be looking at her on one of those some day after she got to Hollywood and was a movie star. We didn't have one of them television sets at our house and weren't likely to get one neither since Preacher Cox, our preacher at Glade Springs Pentecostal Holiness Church where we go, said all that stuff they was putting on there was a sin to watch. Especially them women on there half naked. But this wasn't making no difference to Rachael. She planned to be one of them women just as soon as she could grow up and get out to California. I just couldn't get it through my head how in the world if them folks was all the way out in Hollywood, California, could they be seen in that little box right here in Glade Springs, West Virginia.

Mr. Marshall is the mayor of our fair city, too, but the only time that you can tell it, is when he rides in the Christmas parade in his car with the big sign on the side that says, Mayor Gilbert Marshall. Pap calls him and Sheriff Barnes both 'lected officials, except that one is just for the towns business and the other is for the town and the county's. Pap says the town ain't got one bit of need for a mayor, that it's just a waste of taxpayers money to pay a man just to say whether or not some visiting preacher can set up a tent in the field beside of the ice plant and hold revival. He ain't even got a mayor's office that I know of, I think he just always stays at his office in the back of the furniture store. But if being mayor means you've gotta have a prissy wife, then I reckon Mr. Marshall is the one. Mrs. Betty Marshall is the prissiest thing I ever seen. Why, she won't even walk out of doors if the wind is blowing the least little bit, cause it might mess up her hair. And ever dress she's got, has a pocketbook and high heel shoes and a hat and a belt that all match up perfectly. Whenever we see her over at Maxine's, she's always talking about her shopping trips over in Charleston, and how much she has done paid for a new dress or hat. Well, my mama could have took that much money and made her ten dresses and they'd everone have looked as good as any Mrs. Marshall got over in them fancy stores in Charleston. Now, Maxine can walk and talk just like Mrs Marshall, and just as soon as she leaves out of the beauty shop, Maxine goes prissing across the floor like she's walking in high heels with a purse hanging on her right arm and saying how she's got to get in out of the wind for it musses her hair. Why, I even heard talk that the reason Mrs. Marshall hadn't ever had no younguns is cause she didn't want to get all swelled up and mess up her figure.

Chapter twenty-seven

Across Main Street beside the field where we have the Glade Springs annual picnic, is the Presbyterian Church. That's where most of the folks that live in town, and are a little uppity, go. Like Mr. and Mrs. Barker and the Nichols, and the Marshalls. And next to the church's parking lot is Maxine's Beauty Nook. Now, if you want to know what is going on in Fayette County, that is the place to go find it out. Everbody comes in here to get their hair done, from Mrs. Nichols right on down to Sara Jane Dillon, course Sara Jane only came in that one time that I know of, and even Judy Hobbs, she helped Maxine in the beauty shop then, and didn't come from a family much better than Sara Janes, acted like she was afraid to touch her hair. It was like she thought that Sara Jane might have some of them cooties on her, like them that Mary Beth had seen on the back of Pete Collins' neck. I think all Sara Jane really wanted was just to join in with everbody else cause all she got was her hair trimmed a little bit. She didn't need nothing else done cause her hair was shining clean and she's already prettier than anybody else around these parts

I was in there that day with Mama, and everbody just quit talking and laughing when Sara Jane came in. Maxine finally asked her what she could do for her in a real smart alecky way, and Sara Jane said she wanted for them to cut off about four inches of her hair. Everthing stayed real quite for a few minutes, then Maxine told Judy to go with her to the bathroom. When they came back out, they didn't say nothing, but, when it was Sara Jane's turn, even though Maxine wasn't doing nothing, it was Judy who finally cut her hair. I couldn't say nothing to Sara Jane cause it was after she'd already been shamed, but I wanted to smack Judy Hobbs and all the other women, too, even my mama. You could tell that Sara Jane's feelings was hurt, and I hope it embarrassed Judy real good, when Sara Jane paid her for the haircut and then gave her a tip.

After Sara Jane left, everbody started talking again, and of course it was about her. That's when I heard it was Sara Jane's own daddy that was the daddy to her baby. Well, even after that tip, Judy Hobbs was talking bad about Sara Jane, too, after she had left. But, you know what, one of these days I just might tell Miss Judy Hobbs that them same folks that she was talking mean about Sara Jane with, was saying the same things about her after she went home. That was the last I ever saw of her. It was right after she got her hair cut that Sara Jane decided to leave Fayette County. She was just gone one day. The same day that Mr. Rogers from down at the car dealership left town. I hope she's happy no matter where she's at today.

Chapter twenty-eight

And things weren't any better for miss Judy Hobbs neither. She married Lester Smith, Now Lester is a Smith but he ain't no kin to Dr. Smith at all. And he was plum mean to Judy. He was part of that sorry Smith bunch that lives off highway 41 going towards Bluefield.. Him and his brothers was always in trouble with the law. They was worse than the Whitts cause the actually broke the law stealing, beating up folks and staying drunk and disorderly. And they were older. All of them boys had been in jail from the time they was in the early teens. Sorry, sorry, sorry, is what pap would say if they came around close to us But Judy married him anyhow and had one youngun after another ending up with five little ones.

They say Lester almost starved the whole family to death. He was a good looking man, but wasn't worth his weight in coal. When he made some money he always spent it on liquor and women. He'd come home drunk and beat up on Judy. They say he even beat them young'uns too and never brought home enough food to feed the whole family. A lot of times the young/uns were seen drinking water from their bottles because he would buy whiskey instead of milk. Judy was so skinny that her clothes hung loose on her body. Our church tried to help her but everytime they'd take food and clothes over to the shack they lived in, Lester would gather it all up and sell it for more drinking and running around money. A lot of the folk talked about how he would gather those young'uns when he'd hear that one of the churches was having home-coming or dinner on the grounds and go eat. Everybody felt so sorry for those little boys and girls. You could tell that the older ones, they was girls, were ashamed everytime he would go begging at the churches. Then at Christmas he would go around to all the churches and other places in the county and put down the kids names so they would get stuff from all of them. It was only at Christmas time that the Smith young'uns had all the necessary things that most kids have all the time.

The Fayette county Social services always gave the youngouns something for Christmas too and it made the folks around wonder since they knowd how bad the the family was living, why they wouldn't just step in and take them kids so's that they would be taken care of all the time . Course nobody really knows just how much of the stuff the family actually got to keep cause Lester Smith partied hard and gave all his girlfriend's presents during the holidays. And poor old Judy never had nothing decent to wear, and her teeth were all rotten, She always looked sick and didn't have the strength to do anything, walked around like a old woman, even with being only twenty four years old.

They lived in a old run down shack, it was not ever a real house, down a long dirt road before you get to where Sheriff Barnes' place is. They didn't have no electricity or nothing, just a well. There wasn't any outhouse either that had rotted away years ago. Judy spent all her days running after the youngouns, going through the woods picking creasy greens and mushrooms and other things that they could eat out of the woods.. She didn't have much to do in the shack. they didn't have hardly any furniture just a wood stove and some mattresses laid out on the dirt floor and a couple of old chairs at a table. And of course not having no electricity, they always went to bed at dark. This went on for a long time then Judy just got tired I guess. She couldn't take care of herself much less the kids, so I guess she just gave up. She ran away. People really talked mean about her running off and leaving them youngouns, but most said she did the right thing by them because she knowd that when she left that Lester would have to start acting like a natural daddy and look after them youngouns. But he didn't do that. He'd leave them at home by them-selves or get one of his girlfriends to go there but them women weren't as easy to run over as Judy had been. They might stay for a week or so but they weren't gonna settle for looking after another womans youngons while he ran around and didn't even bother to feed them. After a while, I think there were so many people complaining about those poor babies that Fayette county social services finally done something.

First off, Lester was arrested for not caring for his family. I heard that sheriff Barnes got just a little bit rough on Lester when he actually put his hand cuffs on him and took him down to the jail house. I'm thinking he probably wanted to get real ruff since he knowed about how Lester treated Judy with them living there right behind his property. But he made sure others knowed just how low down and sorry he was. When Lester was tried down at the Fayette county court house, it was full of folks telling stories of how bad Lester was. Anyway he went to prison and them poor youngouns was sent in all different directions. The girls were sent to the Davis Child Shelter by the children's home society. It was run by a United States senator Henry Davis over in South Charleston. The two oldest boys was put in a foster home in Berkley. The littlest boy was crippled up and had always been sickly and "not all there" according to some folk, so they had a hard time finding somebody to take care of him. Finally they just dumped him off over in Huntington at the state hospital, cause they'd take youngons, too. They used to call it " the home for incurables" That's so sad, and I bet he'll never get out of that horrible place.

In the meanwhile, nobody knowes where Judy is hiding or if she's gone off and died from malnutrition. Course that family stays on our prayer list at Glade springs Pentecostal Holiness Church. Just hope God straightens it out for them children's sake.

Chapter twenty-nine

But it's not just Sara Jane and Judy Hobbs that gets talked about at Maxine's Beauty Nook, though. My Aunt Dorothy told me that if you're not there yourself, no matter who you are, you can be the one they're talking about. She don't hold with gossip of no kind, she don't care who it's about. And I know that what she says is true, too, cause they even talk about her when she's not there and that's the sweetest woman that's ever took a breath of life. They can't say nothing bad about Aunt Dorothy herself, but they talk about what a fool she's been all these years to get took in like she was by Edward and those sorry youngouns of His and that woman's.. Not his and Aunt Dorothy;s they never had any children together. And what gets me, is that my own Gram will set right there and agree with them, knowing full well that these same ones are talking about Paps being so lazy and him drinking shine and about Mama marrying my daddy who stays away from his wife and children all the time doing God knows what. I reckon it just don't bother her none if she ain't right there face to face with them that's doing the talking so she don't know for sure who said it.

Now, I have to own up to the fact that I'll sit right there and listen to a lot of that talk at Maxine's, that's how I've learnt a lot about the folks who live here in Greenbriar Valley, especially them that I don't know too well. But, the main reason I love going to Maxine's is cause she has those True Confession and Modern Romance magazines in her shop. I'll get me one and find myself a corner out of everbody's way and read the whole time that I'm there. That's one reason that I hear some things that I really shouldn't know about yet. Somebody will be talking and somebody else will say to remember that little pictures have big ears, then they'll look over at me to see if I'm listening. As long as I am looking down at the magazine, they'll talk a little lower, but they'll go right ahead and tell whatever it was they was going to say. I reckon I might have a gift or something myself, cause I can just keep right on reading and still hear what they talk about, and remember it all. Sometimes, Mama or Gram, which ever one that I went there with, will ask me if I heard what somebody said and I always pretend that I didn't. Usually, when I say I didn't hear nothing, Gram will just chuckle. I think she knows that I hear plenty and I think the reason that she knows is because if it was her, she'd be sitting there reading and listening too.

If what Maxine and them is talking about ain't all the interesting, I can read two or three of them stories in True Confessions or Modern Romance while we're there. I remember when I first started reading in the True Confessions, I thought all them stories was real, and I thought the pictures in there with them was really the folks that it had happened to. It just didn't make a whole lot of sense to me why them people, they all looked like movie stars, was always falling in love with somebody else besides their own husbands and wives or else their husband or wife was always leaving and going off with somebody else. It's like pretty people just can't be satisfied with nobody. They was always crying and fighting or begging somebody to forgive them and then saying they just couldn't help falling in love with their best friend or something else like that. Most of them stories usually ended up with all the people going off with somebody different. Then one day I read this story about this man that drove a truck. He came home and told his wife that he was leaving her to marry some other woman that he'd met when he was on the road. He had too. His wife said she wouldn't give him no divorce, but he just went right off and left them anyway, and started living in sin with this other woman. This scared me to death. Cause it sounded just like my mama and daddy. I'd heard them fussing about Daddy staying gone in his truck so much and I'd even heard Mama tell him one time, when she was mad, that he was working on a divorce.

I was there at Maxine's with Gram that day, and I couldn't hardly wait for Pap to come to pick us up. When he stopped at Tyson's to get some cow feed, I started crying and told Gram that Mama had wrote to True Confessions and that her and Daddy was going to get a divorce and Daddy wasn't ever coming back home again. Gram did that funny thing with her face like she does a lot when she's dealing with us sorta like she don't know if she wants to laugh or cry, and then she told me that them stories were all just made up by writers that work for them magazines and that they weren't real. She promised me that Mama hadn't wrote that story, that it just happened that some person had done made up something that seemed to fit with my mama and daddy. She had a hard time making me believe her at first cause I ask her if them stories in Life Magazine and Saturday Evening Post about Greta Garbo and Betty Grable was true, and she said they was but that Greta Garbo and Betty Grable was real people that knowed about. These people in True Confessions was just pretend folks with pretend names, and those pictures was models posing for them stories to make them seem real. Then I ask her if it was the same with Modern Romance Magazines, was it all just pretend. She said it was.

Well, knowing that them True Confessions stories is not real eased my troubled mind, but I was disappointed that Modern Romance is all make believe, too, cause those are love stories. Most of them's almost like a fairy tale with this girl being in love with this rich handsome man that she don't think would give her the time of day, and then finding out that it don't matter to him one bit if she's a poor girl from over on the wrong side of the tracks, that he'll love her for ever and ever just the way she is. But the ones that really touch my heart are the ones about men that've gone off to war and they'd wonder the whole time if their sweethearts would still be waiting for them when they got back. Then when their ship pulled in, their girls was waiting on the docks and they'd run and jump in their arms, and they'd twirl all around while they kissed them right on the mouth. Sometimes at night, after I make sure that Mary Beth has gone to sleep, I pretend that Albert Paul's in the Army and he's way overseas somewhere thinking about me. Then, he comes back and I'm right there waiting just like them girls in Modern Romance. Then I'll hug and kiss my pillow like it's Albert Paul and get all snuggled down in it like it's his shoulder that I'm laying on, and go to sleep. Now the reason I have to wait until Mary Beth is asleep cause one night I was pretending, and I was just a hugging and kissing and whispering to my pillow, and she ask me why I was talking to Albert Paul when he wasn't even there. I told her to go to sleep. And she did, but the next morning she told Mama about it. I told Mama that Mary Beth had just been dreaming, but I saw Mama roll her eyes.

Chapter thirty

Hall's One Hour Martinizing and Alterations that Mrs. Geneva and Milton Hall run is right next to Maxine's Beauty Nook. I don't recall ever having anything cleaned there cause we always do our own washing and ironing at home. Even in the wintertime, if we can get a day with sunshine, we hook up our wringer washer and fill up two number two tubs, one for the first rinse and one for the final one, and do the laundry. Mama showed us how to separate the clothes out so that in the first wash load we have all whites, like sheets and towels and our white Sunday blouses, and then the next load will be the light coloreds and finally we wash overalls and real dark clothes in the last wash. If it's warm, Mary Beth likes to stand by the washer and let the water that the wringers squeeze out run over her hands and arms. Mama will let her on the first load and when we wring out the rinse water, but she won't let her put her hands in the water once it gets dirty. And she's always hollering at us to be careful cause one time when Barbara Ann was first learning how to wash clothes, she let her hand get caught in the wringers. By the time that Mama got the washing machine turned off, about half of Barbara Ann's arm had gone through them. It was all bruised and sore for a long time, and Barbara Ann used that for a long time to get out of helping with the wash, too.

I liked hanging the clothes on the line in warm weather, but I sure did dread it when it was cold. I've been hanging out the clothes in the wintertime and they'd freeze before I got through putting them all out, and my poor hands would be cold and red and it'd take a long time to get them warmed up again. But in the summertime, I take my time and hang them all just as neat as I can. Mama always keeps plenty of clothes pins, cause with as many as she has she knows it's going to take a plenty, and she made a cloths pin bag that'll slide on the cloths line so you can push it over ever time you hang up a piece, and I like to hang all the same things together so it'll look nice. If it's warm out, we always fold the clothes when we get them off the line, and put them in Mama's big reed basket that Gram made her. Mama always wants to get the clothes ironed on wash day, too. I sure was glad when Barbara Ann got big enough to help with the ironing, cause that's one thing I don't care nothing at all about doing. Gram always tries to make me feel like it ain't much of a chore now. She says that when she was a girl and learned how to iron, that she had to use one of them old irons that we use as a door stop cause they didn't have no electricity on the mountain then, and she had to heat it up on the wood stove. I ain't never used nothing but a electric one, and we have almost a new one too, a present for when Mama got caught with John Issac. The only thing is that we have to unplug the radio to use it, cause we have to use the drop cord, and ironing is really tiresome if you can't hear some music while you're doing it. I'm happy about one thing, at least when Mama showed Barbara Ann how to iron, I got out of doing it a whole lot cause I already did most of the washing. But I do like for my things to be ironed, though, and I especially love going to bed and laying my head on a pillow with a fresh smelling ironed pillow case on it.

It's just the other way around down at Hall's One Hour Martinizing and Alterations, it's better doing laundry in the wintertime there cause they do inside the building and when it's cold the heat and steam from the dryers and irons make it all cozy like in there. But in the summer they still have to do all the work inside and it gets so hot in there that you can't hardly get your breath. Mama goes in there sometimes to help Mrs. Geneva do some alterations when she gets behind. Now, Mrs. Geneva Hall used to live in Philadelphia, Pennsylvania, and she has done some sewing for some real rich people. She learned how to sew when she was just nine years old when she went to work in a factory. Then when she got grown, she met up with Mr. Hall, and he knowed all about sewing, too. His mama and daddy had made clothes for other people all the time, and he had learned how to do it from them. Now both of them know all about clothes and fabrics and how to clean them and sew them. Mrs. Geneva had seen some of our clothes that Mama had made and that's how it came about that Mama helps her with alternations. She's told Mama that she ought to set her up a shop of her own and sew for other folks, not just for her family, and make some money doing it. But Mama says she's got too much to do just raising us and that she don't need no more than what Mrs. Geneva already pays her when she helps her out.

If you look directly across from Hall's One Hour Martinizer and Alterations, you can see down Elm Street. On down that street is where Mr. and Mrs. Barker live in their great big white house that his mama and daddy had, and the Marshall's live almost straight across the street from them. But, back on the corner of Main Street and Elm Street next to Marshall's Furniture Store is where Sheriff Barnes' jail house sets. It ain't a very big jail house. When you first go in, it's a right good size room with two desks setting in it. Mrs. Ross sits at one of the desks and answers the telephone and then she can turn around in her chair and talk in the microphone to call out to the police car. The other desk is where the sheriff and Deputy Ben work off of. You can't see the prisoner's cells when you go in, you have to go through the door in the middle of the front room and then there's one on the right and one on the left. Pap let me see in there one time when me and him went down to the jail house. There weren't no people in there then, as a matter of fact there weren't nothing in them cells at all except a cot and a chamber pot. But it still was scary to me. And while I was looking in one of them jail cells, Ben Walker slipped up behind me and pushed me in and shut the door. I almost cried cause I was so scared and he kept on teasing me and saying I had to stay in there. He finally let me out when I promised him I wouldn't never do anything to have to go to jail for.

Course Ben Walker has no need to worry about me ever getting thrown in that jail cause I'm scared to death of being in there. I had heard the stories about Herman Drenth, the "West Virginia Blue Beard" is what they all called him. He had a place up in Clarksburg and he had built an underground torture chamber where he had killed a lot of people. The way he was caught was that his neighbors smelled horrible odors coming from his place and when the police officers got there they found five bodies buried out in his yard. There was all kinds of things that they found in his dungeon that proved that he had killed people, a lot of people. They say that he made a gas chamber and that's how he would kill the women and he would take a hammer and kill the children, and that when the officers got there, there was still blood and stuff still in the dungeon. That was the scariest part, the children, and ever time I hear anything about this horrible monster, I get scared all over again. Anyway, the reason that I'm scared of our jail is that they say that they brought Herman Drenth over here from the West Virginia State Penitentiary in Moundsville and put him in this jail before his trial because was wanting to kill him. Course the officials killed him themselves after his trial. They hung him. Now, they hung Herman Drenth in 1932, but just thinking that I was in the same cell that he had been in makes chill bumps run all over me. No, Ben don't have to worry about me being put in that cell again and it ain't no wonder to me now that Pap don't want to be locked up in there.

Across the street on the other corner of Main Street and Elm Street is Matthew Jackson's Texaco Fire Chief Service Station. The only time I get to go to the Texaco Station is when Pap has gas put in his pickup, and one time when Daddy was home I got to ride with him in his big truck, and I rode layin up in his sleeper bed, down to the Service Station cause he needed some oil. Samuel Logan works here with Matthew Jackson. They'll come out when you pull up and pump the gas, however much you want goes up in the top of the pump where you can see what it looks like, it looks orange colored and I like to smell it, too, and then they pump it in your truck for you. And they work on cars and trucks over on the side of the Service Station, too. It looks like a dark dungeon down there where they work on them cars, they can get all the way down under neath them, and it's all slick with oil down there. Most of the time, Samuel Logan and Matthew Jackson both look like somebody's smeared oil all over them, even their hair looks oily, what you can see around their caps, and their fingers and fingernails are always black. Even when they're not at the Texaco Service Station, if you get close up to them, they smell like that oil and gas, too, no matter if they look like they've just took a bath and put on clean clothes.

One time down at Jackson's Service Station, it was when he changed it over cause it used to be Jackson's Sinclaire Service Station when Matthew's daddy was still running the place, they had something like a party. They put up that brand new red Texaco Fire Chief gas pump, they'd had a green one when it was a Sinclaire station, with the Fire Chief hat on it and they put up red flags and signs and was giving little drinks of Coca Cola. Just about had a car or truck was there cause they was giving away tokens that you could get twenty-five cents worth of free gas with. And ever one of us got one of them red Fire Chief hats to take home, too. I gave mine to John Issac when he got big enough to play with it. Matthew Jackson was a real friendly man, and he had Samuel to take one of them inner tubes, when it had got where it weren't safe to put in a tire again, and he put big old square patches on it and blew it up and we would get on it and float in the creek where Daddy had dug out a swimming hole for us. It was so much fun, but you had to be careful getting on it so you wouldn't scratch yourself on the stem where it was blowed up at. And he was the one that gave us that tire that Pap took and made us a swing out of, too.

Chapter thirty-one

Next to the service station is three more places all built together like they're one big one building. Dr. Smith's office is the first door you get to. He's the only doctor that I know and he doctors on just about here in Greenbriar Valley. It was his office I was in when I saw that poor crippled up little baby that belongs to Walter and Catherine Jacobs, and he's going to deliver the baby that Mama is carrying now. She is going to go to the hospital in Bickley to have this one, and Dr. Smith plans to be right there with her. When Mama goes to see Dr. Smith for a check-up, he always looks in all our throats and ears and asks us if we have been feeling all right. Usually, the only one of use that has to have any medicine is John Issac and if Dr. Smith gives him a shot, sometimes if his ears are infected Dr. Smith has to give him penicillin, you can hear him yell all the way to Charleston. Mama says that we're all real healthy cause she keeps us cleaned out good. About ever month or so, she goes over to Waverly's Drug Store, Gram says it used to be called the Apothecary Shop, and gets a bottle of Castor Oil and a bottle of Casoria and she gives it to us. She'll mix it up together, so it won't taste so bad, and we hold our noses and try to swallow and not gag on it. Mama says we've got it easy, cause when she was a and Gram dosed her, it was with just pure old Castor Oil.

Dr. Smith vaccinated all of us, too. He tells all the youngouns about how they could get polio and get all crippled up themselves, or either get small pox if they don't get a vaccination. I remember when I got mine that I was scared half to death that it was gonna hurt real bad, but it didn't, so when it was time for all the younger ones to get theirs, I fussed at them for acting like babies. And I could tell them about how I even had to have two smallpox vaccinations cause the first one didn't do right, and I have two scars on my left arm to prove it. Gram says that it's just useless for anybody to be going to a doctor so much. She's always telling how when any of them got sick when they was young how her mam and pap always doctored them themselves. The only time they ever got help, was when it was something real serious like they needed a bone set or some special medicine and herbs. Or if a woman needed help having a baby, then they would go get the granny midwife. That's one reason that Mama will take care of us herself most of time, like when she puts the sweet oil in John Issac's ears or gives us Castor Oil. And most of the women around here still call on Miss Claire when their babies are coming, but last time with John Issac, Mama had some kind of trouble and Pap had to go get Dr. Smith even with Miss Claire's being there, so she thought it best to go on to Dr. Smith and let him take care of things this time just in case.

I probably like Dr. Smith about as much as I can like any man besides my Daddy and Pap, and Albert Paul, of course. He can talk to you in a way that you don't get too flustered about things that a woman needs to know. I remember a couple of years ago when we was in and he was checking us over and he ask me how old I was. When I told him I was eleven going on twelve, he asked me if I had started my period yet. Well, I hadn't yet, but I knowed what he meant and my face turned as red as a pair of Pap's flannels, but he told me it was just a normal thing that a doctor knows all about. He just wanted me to know that when I did start having it, that it meant that I was growed up enough so that I could be a mama, and that sometimes it might make my stomach hurt, and that I might think I was going to bleed to death, but for me not to be scared about it, and to come see him if I had any problems. He told me that he'd took care of me ever since I'd been in this world and that he'd take care of my when they came along. And he said I could come and talk to him about anything I wanted to. Well, even though I told him I would, there's just somethings that I want to know that a woman needs to talk to another woman about. So that's when I go to Gram.

Chapter thirty-two

Gram is the person I always go to if I don't understand something, or if I want to know about something. I reckon when it comes right down to it, that I love my Gram more than anybody else in this whole wide world. I was just real little when me and Mama lived with her and Pap that time, but I can remember it. I can recall sitting in Gram's lap anytime I wanted to. I didn't even have to be sick or hurt or anything, I could just go up to her and she'd pick me up. She'd hug me, tickle me, sing to me or just hold me until I'd go to sleep or want to get down. I could just snuggle right into her, and she was always so warm and smelled like soap powder and Halo shampoo. She'd take me walking in the yard and woods and we'd pick flowers and black berries and wild grapes, and she taught me how to make necklaces out of flowers. When me and mama moved over to her Uncle Rolands house, I cried and cried for my Gram. She came over and stayed as much as she could until I got used to being away from her, and she's always been close by while I've been growing up.

I ain't afraid to ask my Gram about anything no matter what it is, and she'll try to explain it to me, too, no matter what it is, and since I've been twelve, she talks to me like I'm almost a full growed woman. And I can count on Gram to tell me the truth about things, too, even if it's something that I don't quite get the meaning of, I know it's so if she says it. And I can talk to her about whatever comes up, like some of the things that me and Rachael do and talk about. She'll listen and tell me that she understands how I feel. Now, she don't always think it's proper what we do and talk about, she don't hold with just out and out sinning, she's a good God fearing Christian woman, and she thinks some of these things is wrong, but she says she can understand us feeling the way that we feel and wanting to know some things that we are so curious about. Course, there's a lot of things that I don't have to tell her cause she already knows it. Like my being in love with Albert Paul. Why, she said she's knowed that for a long time, and when Mama and them are teasing me about it, she always has something to say back to make them leave me alone. Like she'll recall Mama being in love with that ugly Elmore Whittenly, whose daddy used to work for Mr. Waverly over at the drug store, when she was just twelve years old and the way she would try to act so growny when he came around, and she'd tell Barbara Ann that her times acoming.

Gram can play the piano and sing, too. She's the one that plays the piano at our church and she don't even have to have any music to play by. She says she plays by ear, and she can just hear somebody sing a song and she'll start playing right along with them. And she can sing with near about anybody, too, and harmonize right along with them just like Shorty Moses does. Course the times I liked her singing best was when she was holding me in her lap when I was little, and I'd lay my head over and put my ear right against her chest. I could hear her singing right through her body and it'd make me feel like nothing on God's green earth could ever go wrong as long as she was rocking and singing. I reckon Gram's family was what you call musically gifted cause just about all of them could play something and sing. At Christmas time when all Mama's brothers and sisters and cousins and aunts and uncles would come back home, they'd all sit around at Gram's and that's what they'd do. It sounded better that the radio. I thought that they ought to have gone and made some of them records like the Carter Family, but they'd all laugh and say that folks wouldn't be able to tell them apart.

Poor old Pap, he can't play nothing. But he likes picking and singing about as good as he does coon hunting. One reason's because when all the kin folk come around, most of the time somebody has a jar of moon shine. Now, Gram don't hold with drinking neither, so when Mama's brothers or Uncle Dallas slips it up to the house, they always hide it so Gram can't get her hands on it. I can recall a few years ago when I almost ruined the singing at Christmas time. was there and we'd finished up eating and they'd just started picking and singing, when Gram told me to get her a cold drink of water. The water bucket was almost empty, so I went out to the well purely intending to draw up a bucket of fresh water. When I took the top off the well, I saw where somebody had already put some water in a mason jar and left it in there to stay cold, so taking the easy way, I just pulled that jar right up by its rope and took it right in to Gram. I knowed something was wrong the minute I got back in the room, but I didn't know what it was until I handed Gram that jar and she took the top off. The music stopped right then and there and Gram went out to the kitchen and poured that shine right down the sink drain. I thought the fun was over for sure and I just knowed that Pap would never forgive me for getting his shine poured out, but after a bit, they all just started back up with the music, and Pap winked at me. I think one reason that Pap didn't get no madder at me than he did was that they had another jar hid else. And it didn't take long afore all the men was having to go to the outhouse ever little while. You can always tell when Pap has really got in that moon shine. He'll start clapping his hands and patting his feet and before long he'll break right out and start dancing. He can pure cut a rug, too. He's so tall and skinny, and he's got the longest legs I bout near ever saw, but I'm always scared that if he gets too happy and moving too fast that he's gonna get them legs all tangled up and fall flat on his face.

Me and Pap are real close, too. Even though Gram calls him heathern and a rascal, I like being with him most of anybody out side of Gram. Mama says he's the one that's making me out a tomboy, cause I like going out with him at night and listening to the hounds run a coon, and Pap's always coming by the house and getting me to go with him over to Uncle Dallas' when they're working in tobacco. One of my most favorite things in the world is to go with Pap when he helps haul the tobacco to the market for Uncle Dallas over in Wheeling. They always stay over there for most of the morning, while the tobacco's being sold, and they always have money when we start back home. Pap will pull in to that big Exxon truck stop out on Highway 40, and we go in the cafe part and eat lunch. This is something that just me and him do that's just mine and his special thing. Mama's sister Clo's son, James Jr., they're some of the ones that live over in Low Gap, North Carolina, came up here and stayed for a whole week last summer, and he went with Pap to Wheeling to sell tobacco one day. I was just plum mad, cause I just knowed that he was gonna get to eat at that truck stop in my place. And that was the first thing I asked him about when they got back and he said he didn't know nothing about no truck stop. I reckon I was just being foolish, but I didn't want nobody else going in my place with Pap to that cafe.

Now, I ain't told nobody, but Pap is teaching me how to drive the truck. He says that he knows I'm growing up and it's about time for me to be learning things that will do me some good. We always turn right off of our road and go a ways out Highway 19 where there's a long stretch of flat road for me to practice, cause I have a hard time stopping that truck if we're coming down the mountain. It gets to rolling so fast and I have to almost stand straight up on the clutch and the brake to slow it down. The first time I did that, it scare me so bad that I wouldn't try to drive for a whole week. Finally, Pap said he'd take me to where it weren't so steep and curvey and we found that place out on Highway 19. I'm doing ok now so long as we don't have to go up or down a real steep hill. I've learnt how to let my foot off the clutch easy enough so as not to make the truck jump along when I shift gears, and I know how to give my turn signals. You put your arm straight out the window if you want to turn left and you bend your elbow so your hand is pointing up if you want to turn right. I still have some trouble trying to get that truck to go if I have to stop on a hill, but Pap says it'll all come to me with practice. And I plan to keep right on practicing ever chance I get.

Next door to Dr. Smith's office is Waverly's Drug Store. Old Mr. Waverly is the druggist and he always has on a white coat and he's almost always at the back of the store where you see the red neon sign that says Prescriptions. He's up about two or three steps higher than the rest of the store, and he has to bend over when he gives you your medicine. Now Mr. Waverly has lost just about all his hair on the very top of his head but he still has a bunch on one side. So he combs that hair on the side over his bald spot, I reckon he's ashamed of it and he's trying to hide it, but ever time he bends over to hand you something, that hairs flops right back over to the side showing off that pink shinny head of his. Gram says she don't see why he don't cut off that long hair and glue it where he ain't got none. Donald Gene is Mr. Waverly's son and he always wears a white shirt and suspenders with a little red bow tie, and he works the rest of the drug store, even the fountain. They've got stools up at the counter, they're made out of green leather, and they've three little round tables that are taller than most you see. They all have just two chairs and the chairs are high like the stools at the bar. Most folks feet can't touch the floor when they're sitting on them, they have to hook them in the rungs at the bottom of the chair. You can get sodas and milk shakes and stuff like that at the fountain, and you see a lot of boys and girls who come in there to talk and play the jukebox that Mr. Waverly put in. I've seen William Lee and Edna June sitting at one of them tables listening to music and looking into each others eyes like they was the only folks around, and they was drinking soda out of the same glass with two straws. I can't hardly wait until me and Albert Paul can do like that.

Waverly's Drug Store's the only place that I ever remember seeing Arthur Ray Whitt. He had on his uniform, and I don't know what Mama and Gram and Pap would say if they knowed it, but I though he was just about the handsomest thing I'd ever seen. He wasn't sitting on no stool, he was just leaning up against the bar talking to this girl that I know was in the eleventh grade, but I don't know what her name is, when two of his cousins came in. They had on their overalls and was carrying about twenty pounds of red mud on their boots, just like they always do. They went over there and was talking to Arthur Ray and the girl and before anybody knowed what was happening, Arthur Ray and his cousin named Bennie was wrestling right there in the middle of the drug store floor. We was standing back under where the red neon sign said Prescriptions, Mama was waiting for Mr. Waverly to give her some paregoric for John Issac cause he had the colic, so we didn't hear what had got Arthur Ray so riled up, but he was giving Bennie a whipping and a half until Donald Gene and his other cousin, Gordon, stepped right in the middle of it. Donald Gene grabbed Arthur Ray and Bennie's brother got him, and they held them there until they'd cooled off a bit and was ready to settle down. Mr. Waverly came out from behind the counter and told them to get out of there or he'd call Sheriff Barnes. I still don't know what they was fighting over, Grams says it could've been anything, since them Whitts just like to fight even if it has to be with their own kin. All I know for sure was that Donald Gene had to sweep up all that red dirt that had come off of their boots and was left there on the floor.

Red Davis' Barber Shop is next in line after Waverly's Drug Store. Now I ain't never been in there but one time, and that was to see if Pap was through getting his hair cut and ready to take me and Gram home. The thing that I remember the most about the barber shop, except for Mr. Davis' red hair, well it was really almost orange, was how it smelt in there. Ain't no woman's perfume could've smell any better than what Mr. Davis was putting on them men, and I recall thinking that it looked sorta like Maxine's Beauty Nook, too. It had the same kind of chairs and some sinks like them in the bearty shop, and I would just bet that them men was sitting around gossiping just like all them women do at Maxine's. And I reckon all the men folk around here have to go there to get their haircuts, cause I saw Mr. Nichols, Samuel Logan and Mr. Caleb Whitt all in there at the same time. They was all acting real kindly like, talking to each other, and I know ain't none of them three friends. Something else I remember is the fact of them men in there teasing me about being a boy and coming in to get all my long hair cut off. I reckon they started it cause I had on some overalls cause me and Pap had been over at Uncle Dallas' farm before we went and got Gram and brung her in to town, but they knowed it was me. Mr. John Randall Nichols, II was the most worry some of the whole bunch, course I'm not surprised at that, being as it seems to run in the family. But, I got plum mad at him cause he just kept on saying that girls didn't come in barber shops, so I had to be a boy. I reckon he thought he was being funny, but I thought he was being stupid.

Chapter thirty-three

Directly across Main Street from where Dr. Smith's office, the drug store and barber shop are, is where Penny's Diner is. We get to go in there bout ever time we come in town cause Penny and Mama are cousins, her daddy is Gram's brother George that lives in the old Watt's home place. And a lot of times when we're in there, more of our kin folks will come in and we'll all just sit around and talk and have a real nice visit. Penny's just about the only one of our kin that lives in town. Her and her husband Al live right out back of the diner in one of them trailers of their own. Theirs's don't look like the trailers in Marshall's Trailer Park, though, cause Al has built on to theirs. He made a front room that is as big as the whole rest of the trailer and he put on a porch and a bathroom. And he even built them a garage to put their car in. They use the part of the trailer that is a sitting room in Rachael's like a dining room in theirs, and they tore down the wall that was making two different bedrooms so that it is just one room. Penny's real good about fixing things up pretty, too. She's done made covers and pillows for her funiture, and they have braided rugs all over the floors. It's probably just what me and Albert Paul will do with our trailer after we've been married awhile and start to have younguns and need to have more room.

I like Penny a lot. I think a part of it is we both love animals especially dogs. They have a shaggy dog that ain't nothing except a bunch of curly black hair. She looks a whole lot bigger that she really is, and when you pick her up, why, she don't weigh no more than a feather. They call her their Dolly, and Penny treats her just like a youngun. She even has her own little bed, it looks like a dolls bed, with ruffles on the side and a mattress where Penny puts a blanket for Dolly to sleep on. And toys, Penny has made that dog all kinds of things to play with, more than all us Carver younguns ever had put together. She feeds Dolly steak right from the diner, and it ain't nobody's left overs neither, it's her very own steak, and she makes little outfits and puts them on that dog. I think it's all real cute and sweet they way they treat her, and I like Dolly a lot, but there's just something about a plot hound, and I like them better than any other kind of dog.

Penny's Diner is another one of my favorite places to go. They have a long bar with stools covered in red leather, and they will turn all the way around with you. Sometimes Mama gets on to us when we get on them cause we'll make them spin around, but it's fun and it makes your head feel sort of funny when you stop. And there's booths all the way down the side of the diner. They're red, too, and on everone of the tables there's a salt and pepper shaker, a sugar bowl, a bottle of Texas Pete and some vinegar. Mama usually makes us sit in one of these booths when we eat or drink anything so we want be turning around on them stools. I guess that's a good thing cause we don't have to worry bout the Goat Man sitting down next to us and stinking so bad that we don't even want to drink our Orange Crush. The best thing at Penny's Diner is her ice-cold Orange Crush. It comes in a dark brown bottle, and we drink it through a paper straw, and we like it even better if we can all have our very own bottle and not have to share. We don't eat much at the diner cause we almost always eat our meals at home, but ever once in a while we'll get us a hot dog. Now, they're some good things. You can get Penny to fix them up however you like them, and I always tell her I want mine all the way. When you say you want it all the way she puts mustard, onions, chili and slaw on it and then wraps it up in that thin paper and you can smell that hot dog right through it. It's always so runny that you have to keep that paper wrapped around it white you are eating it, but that's half of what makes it so good. A good old hot dog all the way and a orange crush is pure delight.

Since I've been as big as I am now, when we go to Penny's Diner, Penny will put one of her aprons on me and let me help her wipe off the tables and the bar. And sometimes, I'll help her to fill up the sugar bowls and salt and pepper shakers, but she ain't let me help her cook none yet. She says that I'm still too young to be messing around a hot grill. It probably would be a pretty good job, working in a diner when you've growed up if you don't get to go to college, and I might would do it for a while, till I started to have my young'uns. Then I reckon I'd just as soon stay home and look after them and keep house for Albert Paul.

Chapter thirty-four

When you come out of Penny's Diner and look off to your left, you can see the Glade Springs Pentecostal Holiness Church sitting up on the hill. I figure that if you walked it, it would be about four city blocks away from the diner. It ain't no real fancy brick church like the Presbyterian Church in town. It's built out of wood and it is painted white and it has a cross on the top of its steeple. It looks like a picture post card in the fall when all the leaves on the big trees around the church yard have done turned all different colors, and in the wintertime when it snows, especially at Christmas when they've put them green wreaths with big red bows up on the doors. And when the church bells are ringing, you can hear them all over the town of Glade Springs.

The parsonage sits just a little ways out beside the church, on the side away from the grave yard. This is where our preacher, Brother Hiram Cox and his wife Naomi and their younguns live. Now, this is the second family of Cox's that's lived in that parsonage and preached at our church. Reverend Otis Cox, the one what raised Shorty Moses and Brother Hiram's daddy, was the preacher before him. Him and Miss Molly lived here right on up to the time that Brother Hiram got married to Sister Naomi, he was already doing the preaching at the church and living in the parsonage with his mama and daddy, then they moved in the little house that the church built for them down behind the schoolhouse on Walker Street. Brother Otis Cox still gets up in the pulpit ever once in a while, even though he's getting on in years, and preaches up a storm. But it don't matter which one of them is doing the preaching, our church is always on fire for God. Everbody gets in there during services and especially if we're having revival and they start singing and praying and the blessings just flow straight down from Heaven.

The music is what I love best. Gram plays the piano and Sister Naomi plays an accordian, Shorty plays his guitar, Uncle George, Gram's brother plays the bass and now Penny's husband Al has started playing the drums. That bunch gets to playing, especially if it's a good fast spiritual like There's Power in The Blood, and everbody in there will be on their feet singing and shouting and sometimes speaking in tongues. Even old Pap with his heathen ways will be clapping his hands right along with the rest of them, and I could just listen to it on and on. And, Brother Hiram has a fine singing voice, too, just like his daddy before him. I've seen it when he'd get up to preach his sermon that he'd start singing and it'd end up being a gospel singing instead of preaching with everbody joining in. The music would just keep coming out of us all and we'd praise the Lord for a solid hour or so. Then when the music would wind down, everbody would start testifying and telling all the good things that the Lord has done for them. And, if it just so happened that some lost soul was under conviction and ended up getting saved by the grace of God during the service, why everbody'd be a loving on them and telling how happy they was to have them join in their church family. It was a good time on that hill in the Glade Springs Pentecostal Holiness Church on them days like that.

And homecomings are pure pleasurable. Ever year at about the same time, all the folks that are members of Glade Springs Pentecostal or if they'd been members even a long time ago, they'd bring their whole family and come for dinner and singing on the grounds. Table and chairs would be set up out underneath the big old oak trees around the church and everbody will bring the food that they was best at cooking and spread it all over them tables. Brother Cox says the blessing and then you can go around and choose what you like to eat best of all and just fill your plate plum full of it. Most of the older folks will sit around the tables and some of the others brings blankets or quilts to sit on and eat. Once the eating is over, they'll start the gospel singing. Usually at homecoming, Gram won't be playing the piano cause it's done outdoors and they can't move the piano out in the yard. But she'll get hold to a tamborine and while all the rest of them are playing, she beat that tambourine slap to death. Sometimes they'll keep right on with the singing throughout the whole afternoon and then pick up them instruments and move back into the church just in time for Sunday evening worship service to start.

Now in church is one place where me and Albert Paul can sit together without nobody saying anything, cause we're in the same Sunday School class, and when Sunday School's over and we go back into the sanctuary of the church, we're all supposed to go in single file and sit on the same bench. I always get in line in front or behind Albert Paul, it depends on who's on the other side of me, and when we go in the church we're sitting right side by side. He always lays his arm up behind my head on the pew, and we look just like all them other married couples sitting throughout the church. We don't talk or hold hands or nothing though, cause Brother Cox keeps a eye out for any hanky panky going on in his church. But that's alright, just sitting there that close to Albert Paul in the house of the Lord is plum near going right on up to heaven on high.

Chapter thirty-five

I already told you what a fine man Brother Otis Cox is, when he took in that poor little orphaned Shorty Moses after he was left on his door steps, and I'm here to say that his son is just as fine a person as his daddy is. If anybody gets sick or is dying because they're old, Brother Hiram will go from one end of the county to the other just to pray for them. And he'll stay right there too in their time of grief if a loved one passes on. His heart must be the same size as Sheriff Barnes' even though he ain't nearly as big as the sheriff is. But he cares about folks and he wants to be there to help comfort them. Just like when Uncle Dallas had his operation, Brother Hiram was right there in that hospital all the way over in Beckley, and he stayed by Auntie Lil's side until the doctor came out and said that Uncle Dallas was going to be just fine. He's always visiting the shut ins, too. Before Nannie O'Brian and Sarge was took off to the nursing home, he went up there every Sunday afternoon and talked and prayed with the poor old things, and I know that he goes to see old Mrs. Schmit and she ain't never even set foot inside the doors of Glades Springs Pentecostal Holiness Church. And the most surprising thing is that he goes to see the Dillons even with the way folks talk about them, and the Whitts, and they have their very own church up on the mountain. Brother Hiram goes over to the Dees' a lot but it don't surprise me none that him and Mr. Dees is such good friends. They are about the same age and they growed up together here in

Fayette County. They talk about running these mountains playing cowboy and Indian and then fishing and hunting when they got older. They were at each other's weddings and after they both got older started their fishing and hunting together again. Brother Hiram don't care what other folks says about them being different. He loves his Brother Dees . As a matter of fact, he loves everbody. He don't care who they are, where they come from, what color they are or what they might have done, they're all still God's children and he says that he loves everone of the Lord's creations. And he told the whole congregation that when he goes and visits all these folks, that he always invites them to come worship in our church. And he says that if they ever do, that his flock had better make them feel welcome.

Brother Hiram goes to all the wakes of the folks in his church and he even goes to some who ain't members of our church, too. He was there all night when Mama's brother Roland was laid out. I ain't been to too many wakes besides that one except Mama's brother, my uncle Gerald and when my baby brother Charles Garland died just one day after he was born. And I don't recall what all went on that time cause I was just six years old myself, and I went off to sleep while all the folks was still at our house. But I remember all about Uncle Gerald's wake. I stayed up all night with the rest of the folks and everbody kept going in and out and eating and then different folks would come in and stay awhile and then leave. Brother Hiram was there when they opened up the coffin and he was the one that closed it for the final time. He preached Uncle Gerald's funeral, too. We all went to the church and they put Gerald right up in front of everbody while Brother Hiram talked about what a fine family that Gerald Cole had come from, and he prayed that when this fine family got to heaven that Gerald would be standing right there beside Saint Peter at the Pearly Gates to welcome everone of us in. Then they carried him out and buried him right beside where Gram said that her old bones would spend eternity. Gerald's got his very own tombstone, and my baby brother does, too. His says on it: Charles Garland Carver, Born April 8, 1940, Died April 9, 1940. A Little Lamb of God. And it has a little lamb laying right on the top of the tombstone. When I look at little Charles' grave site, I can't help it that a tear comes to my eyes ever time.

Of course, Brother Hiram does weddings, too. Between him and his daddy, they must have married about ever member of my family, as least them that was married in church. I've heard my mama ask my daddy if they could get married again at the church, they ran off and got married some-where down in Bennettsville, South Carolina, and they never had a church wedding. And I don't reckon they ever will neither cause Daddy says that him and Mama are just as married all ready as they would be if the went through that big to do at the church. Brother Hiram's going to marry me and Albert Paul though. I've all ready got it all planned out. I'm gonna be wearing the most beautiful long white wedding dress that my mama can make and I'm gonna have one of them long veils like I've seen in them Bride magazines. I'm gonna be holding wildflowers tied with a satin ribbon and when my daddy walks me down that isle, Albert Paul will be standing there beside Brother Hiram in his new black suit and he'll just be shocked plum out of his skin at how beautiful I look. All my sisters, and Albert Paul's sister, Polly will be brides' maids, Rachael will be my matron of honor, John Issac and the new baby, if it's a boy, and William Earl will be ushers. Gram will play the wedding music and the church will be decorated with white ribbon and pink and white flowers and candles. And when Brother Hiram pronounces us man and wife, Albert Paul will kiss me on the mouth right there in front of everbody, and then we'll run down the isle, while they all throw rice at us, to start our married life together. But that's a ways down the road.

Chapter thirty-six

To the left of Penny's Diner is Glade Springs' only place you can buy a new car. The Buick/Chevrolet dealership was run and owned by Richard Harold Rogers. Mr. Rogers, his wife, Gloria and their four children lived in town in a really nice big house. She is so pretty She has big brown eyes and long blonde hair and a shape that the boys call a figure eight. And she likes to show it off with her tight-fitting pedal pushers and hers blouses were cut off way above her waistline. Everybody likes her. She is the fourth-grade teacher at Glade Springs School, and is the school nurse and is there to help anybody that needs her. All of us really like her and If you need to talk about some personal problem she will talk to you. Of course there's always somebody that's gonna say something against everybody and just cause she was so nice didn't stop the gossips There was talk that said she almost got fired from her nursing job one time cause she gave a eleventh grade student some birth control. One of the Whitt girls had done fell in love with a grown up man that already had himself a wife and baby.. She couldn't help herself though, she just loved him so much. But she wanted to graduate eleventh grade this year so she certainly didn't want to get kicked out of school for having a young'un. And was just plum lucky that she had not already got knocked up. Mrs. Rogers talked with her and they said she begged and cried for something so's she wouldn't have no baby. I heard that Mrs. Rogers had to go to be tried by a court of law in the

Fayette County courthouse, but I didn't hear if she was . I just know that Mrs Rogers said she didn't do it. She didn't get fired and as far as I know, the Whitt girl didn't have no baby . Mrs. Rogers didn't act like she was too worried about the whole thing. She just kept on teaching and nursing and didn't even seem to notice when Mr Rogers started acting so funny.

I guess it must of shamed Mr Rogers a lot though, cause it wasn't too long until he stopped being a part of our friendly community. You never saw him with his pretty wife and younguns, not even at the town picnic. If you went by the dealership after dark, you could see him sitting inside in his office. He did this for a long time then begin going to the bars over in Mount Hope. They say while he was there that he was drinking whiskey and talking with a woman that he would meet over there. When you'd see him outside the dealership, he would just walk by and didn't have anything to say to anyone. Seemed sad? I guess this went on for a while and then one day he was gone. Just packed up his bags, took a car off the lot and left Glade Springs. Nobody has heard from him since he left town that day, but it's been told that on that very same day that Mr. Rogers left town a bright red 1941 Chevrolet Coup pulled out of the driveway of Mr. Dwayne Lee Dillon and headed toward Charleston.

Chapter thirty-seven

Fayette County Tribune our local Newspaper is beside the car dealership building. Mr. Reginald Alan Porter is the editor and owner of the Tribune. They say his family was the richest in the county. Not only do they own the newspaper, but the family owns that big old mansion, the plantation as it was known as at the intersection of highways 19 and 41. The largest farm anywhere around here, and at one time they had fine Tennessee walking horses there for sale. They even had a great big riding ring where folks would come and bring theirs horses and ride to see who had the best horse. We went out there and watched the horses go around the ring. They were all so beautiful. These people had their horses all dressed up. Their manes and tails were long and flowing and they had the most beautiful way of walking with their heads bobbing up and down. I especially like one that was old Mr. Porter's horse. His name was Go boy Joco. He was solid black with four white legs, they are called stockings, and a wide white blaze in his face. When they got him ready for his show they put a long artificial tail on him, braided his long mane with red ribbons and put white boots on his feet. He wore a shinny black saddle and a bridle with a red headband , and the man that rode him was dressed up in one of them tuxedos that you see in magazines. They won a lot of trophies and Reginald Porter was always there to get a picture that was put on the front page of the Tribune.

If there were events going on anywhere, your saw Reginald Porter bent over under that big old camera on his back and his note pad sticking out of his pocket. He was going to find a story wherever he went and if lucky a picture to go with it. And you could count on a whole page of pictures after the Glade 'spring picnic. He wrote about everybody and everything that he could find and put it in the Fayette County Tribune. If you got married, it was in the tribune, If you died, you were there and especially if you got in any kind of trouble. Why you'd probably make headline. Old Mr. Porter had run the Fayette County Triune since 1908 and they had reported on some really big stories over the years. Like when the town of Mount Hope burned to the ground. And they had printed every name of all the men and boys killed in the mind that blew up. They one where Nannie and Sarges men folk had all been killed. He wrote about the house fires that killed Edward and his woman and about when Mr. Wood burned his down. And the story about Author Ray Whitt when he was killed in the war. But one I recall for sure, cause everybody still talks about it, is about the suspicious red vehicle that pulled out the Dillions driveway and drove towards Charleston the day that Mr. Rogers and Sarah Jane Dillon disappeared.

Don't know a lot about Reginald porter himself except that he is married to Lucille Porter. They live in the plantation and had two boys, Martin and David. David was in my class at school. Now he really is smart not pretend smart like John Randal Nickols lll and he don't show off and act biggity even though he is rich. And Martin seems nice too even though he's still little. You don't see Lucille out much, she seems shy but you might see her out in the park reading a book almost any pretty day She almost never talks with anyone. Not Reginald, though. If you want to talk then he'll talk with you. Never met a stranger Pap said and as friendly a man as you ever want to see. But you'd better watch out cause if you ever did something that he could write about he would. If it was good ok if not you were just told on.

Chapter thirty-eight

If you were to look straight across Main Street from the Pentecostal Holiness Church, you can see our schoolhouse. Gram said it used to be called the Glade Springs Institute of Learning, but now it's just plain Glade Springs School and I've been going to school there from the first grade on. Our school is a real old one, you can hear your footsteps echoing down the hallways when you walk, and the boards squeak too. they're planning to build us a brand-new brick schoolhouse starting next year. They're gonna have to make it bigger cause starting next year we're gonna have twelve grades to go to instead of just eleven like it's always been, and we've got more people going here now since some has moved in since the war is over. They built us a gym about a year ago. It's built out of brick, too, so I reckon our new school will look like it does. I play guard on our girls' basketball team in our new gym, course they make us all play whether we want to or not. I don't mind playing basketball, but I wish they would let me play forward sometimes. All you do when you're a guard is to try to get the ball away from the other team's forwards and give it to the forwards on your team, and you can't even chase them except halfway across the basketball court. You don't ever get to shoot the ball at the basket, that's what I don't like about it most of all. It looks like they'd let everbody go all over the court and if you wanted to, to shoot the ball at the basket. There ain't nobody that I've seen yet can get it in the basket evertime they shoot it, so it looks like they'd give everbody a chance to try it. The only thing I really like about gym class is that they make us wear gym suits. Now, they look like a pair of coveralls that somebody has cut off the sleeves and legs, and there's elastic in the legs and they're short just like a pair of drawers. I always look at myself in the mirror in the locker room after I put on my gym suit, and I like the way my legs look hanging out of that suit. This is the only time us girls can wear shorts out where anyone can see us. And Albert Paul likes the way I look, too, cause when he saw me in the gym that time, the boys ain't allowed in the gym when the girls are having class, but his teacher had sent him down with a note for out gym teacher that day, he whistled and smiled real big at me.

Now everday when William Earl pulls the bus in the parking lot at school he stops it in the same place. Then he makes us sit in our seats until he says we can get off. Course Edna June jumps up and runs up front so she can walk in with William Earl, and that's just fine with me cause then Albert Paul comes up the isle and squeezes my shoulder when nobody is looking. Me and him and Rachael all walk into the school together and go on up the stairs. The first grade through the sixth grade are all on the first floor and the seventh on up to the eleventh are upstairs. Me and Rachael are both in Miss Sadie Covington's six grade class and our room in the last one on the right-hand side when you go in the front door. I like this room cause it's on the side next to Main Street and when you look out the windows, you can see ever thing that's going on over most of the town. We sit at the back of the classroom next to the windows and we get to sit beside each other cause we are almost always good and don't get in no trouble. We don't talk when we're not suppose to neither, cause we don't want to get caught and have to move to the front of the class. Sometimes, if it's just so important that it can't wait, we will pass a note. But we're always real careful so nobody will see us. And we especially always watch out for John Randall Nichols III, cause if he was to see us pass a note, I just know that he would shout it out for the whole wide world to hear.

I love Miss Covington. I don't know how old she is, but she's younger than my mama, cause Mama told me so, and she's pretty and sweet, too. Maybe just a little prettier and sweeter that Mrs. Rogers. I want to be a teacher just like her when I grow up and get out of college, before me and Albert Paul start our family of course, and I think I want to teach the seventh grade, too. We do a lot of reading in here, and I love it. Miss Covington assigns us a book report due ever month that school is in, so I get to spend a lot of time in the library, and I usually wind-up helping Rachael do her book reports, too. It ain't that she ain't smart, she just hates to read anything except them magazines that I got her started looking at. But then, she ain't planning on going to college like me, she's gonna be a movie star, so I guess she'll learn about as much as she needs to know from them magazines. My favorite author is Mr. Charles Dickens. I have read Great Expectations three times and I don't ever get tired of it. I did one of my book reports on it and I made a A+. The only thing about that story is that it is so sad. Poor old Pip gets treated real bad by Estelle, cause her and old Mrs. Haversham want to break his heart, and the old lady is crazy as a loon. But it is so romantic. I know its just a story but I just don't think anyone could wear the same old dress everday for 30 years like she did no matter who it was they loved..

I make good grades in all my subjects, mostly all A's, and that's one reason why me and John Randall fight so much. He always wants to be first at everthing and my grades are usually higher than his is and it makes him mad. I think it's cause he can't go bragging to his daddy that he got the best marks of anybody in our class and he don't get his dollar, that's what his daddy gives him evertime he brings home the highest grade. I don't care if he never gets another dollar, I'm gonna study hard as I can so I can get me one of them scholarships that Miss Covington has told me about. She says that if your grades is high enough, that some folks from them institutions of higher learning will come around and pay your way to go to college so you can be whatever it is you want. She says that I'm smart enough to get to go where I want to college, but she knows just like I do that my folks don't have enough money to send me away to college for four years of extra schooling. That's why she told me about scholarships. I was so excited when Miss Covington first told me about these scholarships that I couldn't wait to talk to Mama about it. But Mama didn't get all excited about it. She told me I might as well just get them high for looting ideas out of my head cause there ain't no way that her and Daddy will ever have that much money to just throw away just cause I had some biggity ideas about going to college, and besides there weren't no use for a woman to get a fancy education when all she needed to know was how to keep a clean house, cook and raise her younguns. She said I'd better just get used to the fact that I was going to stay right here in Greenbriar Valley, West Virginia.

Well, maybe Mama is right. Maybe I will wind up right here in Greenbriar Valley raising young'uns, and I do want to marry Albert Paul someday. But I don't see why a woman can't go to college and learn how to be a teacher and still know how to be a good mama, too. Well, I wasn't gonna argue with Mama about it cause it'd just get me smacked in my smart alec mouth for sassing and it wouldn't get me no scholarship neither. But I talk with Miss Covington about it all the time and she says that she'll offer me all the encouragement that she can. She's done told me that I can be whatever it is I want to be, that I don't have to be a teacher neither, that I can even be a writer like Charles Dickens if that's what I want. At first I thought that Miss Covington was just exaggerating her encouragements when she told me that I could be a writer, but she said that I wrote real good in my book reports and that I had a good imagination and if I would try real hard that I could do it. She told me that I should start right now while I was still in the sixth grade, that I ought to start writing down my memoirs. And she offered me even more encouragement when she told me that if I was to write down my memoirs and bring them in for her to read, that she would give me extra credit on my English grade for it. I ain't never even thought about writing books before Miss Covington told me that, but it sure would be something if I could do it, and that extra credit might just help get me a scholarship.

Epilogue

Mrs. Bradshire let the yellowed pages of notebook paper fall over on her chest. There was a slight tremor to her lips and tears ran down her cheeks escaping beneath closed eyelids as the memories so vividly ran through her mind. Lying there, she could feel the warmth from the old wood stove in their kitchen and smell the homemade bread baking in its oven. She could plainly see her mother's swollen body in her apron and house shoes and the faces of each of her brothers and sisters as they sat around that long wooden table. Barbara Anne, who had married Robert Lee Barnette and had had one son of her own, was still living in the old Barnette house. Sweet Mary Beth, had married David Porter, the oldest son of Reginald Porter, the owner and editor of the Fayette County Tribune our local newspaper, and they had Sally. They had lived in Charleston and both were enjoying retirement. Laura Kate, was widowed and living with one of her daughters in Austin, Texas. John Issac, so much like Pap, remained on the mountain in the old home place, and is still there today. And James Walter, the baby boy born after she had written her memoirs for Miss Covington, is living in Norfolk, Virginia, where he is anxiously awaiting the return of his oldest son from Pakistan.

Gram and Pap, both in the Watts family plot at the Glade Springs Pentecostal Holiness Church cemetery, with Gram lying beside her son Roland, had lived long enough for her to finish college. And they were there to see her father walk her down the aisle to marry, not Albert Paul Ross, but Allan Wayne Bradshire whom she had met at the University of North Carolina at Greensboro. She had, indeed, won a scholarship, thanks to hard work and encouragement from her teachers, and despite her mother's doubts and fears, had received a master's degree after four years at the university. She had returned to teach her own sixth grade class at Glade Springs School and had continued to teach in Fayette County for the next thirty-five years. Her best friend Rachael had quit school before they finished the eleventh grade and had gone to California. She never became a famous movie star, but she had succeeded in securing a few minor parts in several movies before she gave up her dream and went to live in North Carolina. They had stayed in touch for a while, but it had been years now, since she had heard from her.

Most of the people living in Fayette County, described by Mrs. Bradshire in this her first attempt at writing, were now dead, but all had come alive for a brief period as she read. She had once more been at the annual picnic where she listened to her mother play the autoharp while her father sat adoringly at her feet. She could see Shorty Moses strumming his guitar that was as large as he was, and Mr. Dees patting his foot in time with the music as he played his fiddle. And she heard Jennie Lou singing "Amazing Grace How Sweet the Sound" while everyone stopped to listen to her clear sweet voice, and then began to sing along. She tasted ice cold lemon aid deliciously made by Mrs. Edna Osborne and watched the Webbs, Whitts, Dillons, Dees', Nichols, Hunts, Porters, Barnes and Coles all put aside their differences and enjoy the day together. She remembered the precious face of the Abbot baby as Sheriff Barnes had cradled him in his hugh arms. And she remembered Albert Paul Ross.

Albert left the valley at about the same time that she did. He hadn't gone to college, but instead, enlisted in the Navy. There were some letters exchanged for a while, but she had only seen him a few times over the years when he had come back to the mountain to visit his family, and by then, both had married someone else. Whether or not he had children of his own, she had never known. She did know that he had served in the Korean Conflict, and he was one of the first men from Fayette County, West Virginia, to be killed in the war with Viet Nam.

She thought back to when she had married Alan, then a lawyer, and they had bought the house on Elm Street that had once belonged to the Barkers.

How she'd had to grit her teeth when they went to the bank and their loan had to be approved by John Randall Nichols, III. Alan had taken over the Attorney's office, too, when Mr. Barker retired and built himself a little cabin up on the side of Big Walker Mountain close to Gram and Pap's place. And she and Alan were members of the Glade Springs Pentecostal Holiness Church when the third generation of Cox's took over the pulpit.

Over the years the town had grown so, that she had no idea how many streets and new businesses had been built. The flour mill and ice plant had been torn down years ago, and an apartment complex now crowded over onto the field where the annual picnic had been held, and where Tyson's General Store had been, was a Walmart Super Store. Penny's Diner and Maxine's Beauty Nook had both been replace by one large Centura Bank and Hall's Cleaners had been torn down and a McDonalds stood in its place. The brick building that had housed the old bank, attorney's office, Marshall's Furniture and Schmit's Bakery had been used by many different small businesses over the years. Secondhand stores, a record shop and Chinese take-out, just a few. And the jail and mayor's office were located in the courthouse that now occupied the entire corner block of Main and Elm Streets. Gone, were Dr. Smith's office, the barber shop and the old hardware store, and the Texico Fire Chief Service Station had been replaced by several convenient stores located throughout the town. The churches had survived and had been joined by several others of different denominations and the railroad, although not as frequently, was still in use.

Ancestors of the Whitt, Cole, Watts, Dees, Dillon and Barnes families still lived in the valley, but no longer dominated the population, while others, like Marion Moorefield, Miss Claire, and Shorty Moses were just legends talked about by a few older residents of the county. Rebecca no longer personally knew the Sheriff of Fayette County nor the man who held the office of mayor of Glade Springs. She had spent very little time getting acquainted with new neighbors or keeping up with local affairs over the past decade, and now due to her unfortunate accident, she would have to depend on visiting relatives and friends to keep her abreast of the happenings in and around her hometown.

After retirement she had traveled, mostly on the American Continent, but she had visited, a few major countries of the world. And in between trips, she had written several novels to add to a long list of children's books that were published while she was still teaching. Her traveling days where over, but Mrs. Bradshire would still write. It was the thing that she loved best, and she planned to continue as long as her mind remained clear and she could sit at a computer and look out at the mountain and her beloved New River. And, she knew it had all begun with a little encouragement to compose this booklet of notebook paper, handwritten and held together with a pink ribbon, that she now held clutched to her breast.